Choose Me

Silver Fox Romance book #1

Natasha Moore

Choose Me

A Silver Fox Romance novel

Eve Corcoran hates being a cliché, but after her husband leaves her for a younger woman, she's surprised how much she enjoys being on her own. When the empty nester hires the contractor next door to renovate her new apartment, her surprising feelings for him threaten to turn her new life upside down.

After Rick Best lost his wife, he never expected to fall in love again, especially not with the mother of his daughter's best friend. He's gone on enough rescue calls with the volunteer fire department to know life can change forever in an instant, and he can't understand why Eve resists grabbing a second chance at happiness.

Rick wants her to choose a life with him, but Eve is holding on tight to her newly-found independence. As she keeps pushing Rick away, however, being on her own starts to feel a whole lot like being lonely.

Chapter One

The blare of the fire siren sent his blood pumping. It always did.

Rick Best turned his dusty pickup around and tore out of the job site. He'd stopped by the Perrin place after he left the office for the day. One of the crews was finishing up the addition for the out-of-town owners and he wanted to make sure there'd been no problems. At least that's what he'd told himself.

So what if he was putting off heading home. There was no reason to hurry anymore. Hadn't been for a long time now.

The notification tone sounded on his cell phone. It came over as an EMS call, an eighty-seven year old female needing emergency medical service – no response to an emergency alert callback. The job site happened to be just around the corner from the fire hall, so he was the first to arrive. He jumped into the ambulance, pulled it out of the bay and waited for the rest of the crew to arrive. With the app on Rick's phone, he could see which members of the volunteer fire department were responding, so he knew two were on their way. No EMTs yet.

Rick bit back a groan. They were required to have

an emergency medical technician, either on the rig or responding to the scene, before they could roll. Too often they were held up while they waited.

A mud-covered pickup roared into the parking lot, blue light flashing. Ben Krasinski had worn a Captain's hat for a couple of years now and his friend, Joe Waterman's polished black truck was close behind. Still no EMT was showing, though. Rick was just about to contact county dispatch and ask them to call the neighboring department for mutual aid, but then Shelley Gibson's name popped up. She was responding to the scene.

"Let's go," Rick called out as Ben hopped into the jump seat. Joe climbed into the back.

Ben radioed dispatch to let them know they were on route, then flipped the switches for the lights and siren as Rick pulled out onto Main. Flags still lined the street from the Fourth of July parade the past weekend.

The village of Best Bay lay along a four-mile stretch of Lucy Lake in southwestern New York State. The lake community was a combination of upscale summer homes owned mostly by out-of-towners and more modest year-round homes for local families. There were also several apartment buildings within their fire district strictly for the fifty-five-plus crowd.

Rick wasn't thrilled to know that as of his last birthday, he qualified for senior housing.

Shelley was just getting out of her SUV when he pulled the ambulance into the parking lot of the three-story building. Her long blond ponytail bounced as she jogged over from the far end of the parking lot, go-bag in her hand. Sure would be nice if these parking lots were bigger. He'd been here enough times to know there was a rear entrance so he didn't have to worry about turning the rig around in the tight space.

They dashed up the stairs to the third floor. At least

the apartment was right at the top of the stairs and they didn't have to run down the long hall too.

No one was waiting for them to arrive, but if an elderly person had collapsed, perhaps unconscious, she wouldn't be waiting at the door. Rick knocked. No answer. He tried the handle. Locked.

"Shit. Hope we don't have to hunt down the building manager," Ben grumbled. He pounded on the door.

The door flew open to an elderly woman, breathing heavily, her abundant pale skin covered only by a bra and underpants. She froze, the eager expression of anticipation melting from the wrinkled face. "What are you doing here?"

Shelley pushed through with her medical gear. "Ma'am, we got a call that your emergency alert was activated and you didn't respond to the follow-up call. We need to make sure you're okay."

She looked flustered, that was the only word Rick could come up with. "Of course, I'm okay. I must have taken the darn thing off when I..." Her eyes widened as she must have realized how she was dressed. Or rather, undressed. She stomped through the bedroom doorway at the end of the living area. She came back with a robe and the emergency alert necklace in her hands. "It was under the blanket. I must have sat on it."

Rick stood at the door with Ben and Joe. Ben, the officer-in-charge, scribbled on the response form on the clipboard. That was one reason Rick didn't want to run for any leadership positions in the fire department. He was buried in paperwork every day for the business, he sure didn't want any more.

He turned to stare as the woman replied to Ben's request for her name. Sarah Crandall? Rick did a double take. His kindergarten teacher? It was difficult not to run into people you knew on calls in a small town. But that was one image he really didn't want attached to his childhood memories.

"Why are you still here?" Mrs. Crandall asked, propping her hands on her generous hips. At least she'd put the robe on. "Can't you finish your paperwork outside?"

"Yes, Ma'am." Ben had probably had her as a teacher too.

"We just wanted to make sure you're okay." Shelley was too young to have had this woman as her teacher, so she was spared the associated memories. "Would you like me to take your blood pressure? Your face is a little flushed."

"I told you I'm fine. Now shoo." She waved them toward the door. "You have to get out right now. My boyfriend's going to be here any minute!"

Rick held back his laughter until the door closed behind them and they were headed down the stairs. "Boyfriend?" Joe and Ben joined him in the laughter. Just the thought of an eighty-something man, hell, any grown man, being referred to as a *boy*friend, made Rick shake his head. Humiliating.

Ben tucked the clipboard beneath his heavily tattooed arm. "She must have thought it was him at the door when we knocked."

Joe smirked. "Bet those granny panties will really do it for him."

"I say good for her," Shelley snapped. "And good for him. Bet none of you guys have a woman waiting for you to come in the door tonight."

The thirty-something nurse shut them up with that.

After they returned to the hall and the other guys had left, Rick still didn't see any reason to rush home. He washed the rig, even though it didn't really need it. Then he took advantage of the soap and water to wash the dust off his pickup.

When he had nothing else left to do, Rick headed home. He and his brothers had taken over the reins of Best Brothers Builders the previous year when their father, the last remaining original Best brother still in the business, had finally retired. Some days Rick thought he'd be right behind him. He loved the business, but not enough to work until he was in his eighties. But what the hell would he do with his time if he didn't have work?

Oh yeah, some days being a first responder for the Best Bay Volunteer Fire Department took up more time than BBBuilders.

He pulled into the driveway of the large colonial he'd lived in for nearly thirty years. It used to be filled with love and laughter, but his little girl was all grown up and a married woman now. And his wife was no longer waiting for him to come in the door at the end of the day.

Thanks to a drunk driver, they'd been robbed of the chance to grow old together.

The sun was still beating down and he wiped the sweat from his brow. He tried never to complain about the heat. Western New York wasn't known for its hot weather. Still he looked forward to getting inside to the air conditioning and grabbing a beer.

Rick glanced over to the house next door. He liked to keep an eye on it since the husband moved out, the son got a job out west, and the daughter just moved in with her fiancé. He wondered if Eve heard her footsteps echo off the walls like Rick did when he walked into his empty house.

***

"Do you think Amy will kill me if I don't go to the wedding?" Eve Corcoran took a long sip of her Chardonnay and watched her two friends over the top of her glass.

Neither Tess nor Maggie said anything for a moment, just sat there gaping at her from the corner booth at O'Neill's where they had dinner together every Wednesday night. The cozy restaurant offered an eclectic menu and a well-stocked bar, which made it the perfect place for them to meet. Eve cleared her throat and placed her glass carefully on the table.

Finally Tess raised a sculpted brow and dryly replied, "You're the mother of the bride. I think she expects you to show up."

"I know. I know. Stupid question."

"Why don't you want to go?" Maggie asked softly. Her warm green eyes shone with compassion.

Wasn't it obvious? "Don will be there. With Tiffany." Eve's stomach twisted. "I'll be damned if I'm going to show up alone."

"There's nothing wrong with going alone." Tess's dark eyes flashed. "You don't have to have a date to go to your daughter's wedding."

"Yeah, yeah, I know. I just hate being a cliché and everybody knowing it."

"Your husband leaving you for a younger woman does not make you a cliché," Maggie told her. "It makes you a smart woman who kicked him out on his ass."

Eve couldn't help but smile as she remembered chucking a crystal vase and watching it smash against the bedroom wall just inches from Don's head. Okay, so maybe that reaction was a great big cliché, but the satisfaction she felt from seeing the fear cross the cheating bastard's face was worth it.

"I ran into them tonight." There was no reason to tell her friends that she'd ducked into the doorway of Westley's Wine and Spirits, so they wouldn't see her. If she hadn't been headed here, she'd have picked up a big bottle of wine to take home with her.

"Ran into them? With your car, I hope."

She rolled her eyes at Tess's dry comment. "No, walking here from the shop. They'd just come out of Cara's dress shop." Eve wished she could un-see Tiffany with her long thin legs and short tight skirt, snuggling up to Don, giggling as he juggled several shopping bags and a long dress bag. "He never went dress shopping with me."

"Stop feeling sorry for yourself," Tess snapped. "You wouldn't want him dress shopping with you, and you know it."

"You're right. And I'm not feeling sorry for myself. I'm still adjusting, that's all. I like where I am right now." And if she said it enough times, maybe she'd eventually believe it.

"I'll drink to that," Tess said, raising her glass.

After another sip of wine, Eve said, "I'm definitely not looking for another relationship right now. Maybe never again. But I just don't want to walk into that church alone. Is that shallow of me?"

"Not at all." Maggie sent her a small smile. "We'll figure it out. There have got to be a lot of guys you could ask to be your date for the wedding."

Ask? Just the thought sent knots fisting in her stomach. Almost worse than the thought of showing up alone while Don and his new wife threw their happiness in her face. "I don't think I could do that."

"Sure you could. I bet Tess does it all the time."

"Piece of cake." Tess cocked her head toward the tall young waiter carrying drinks to the table next to theirs. "How about him? Bet he'd love to go to the wedding with you. Free food? Drinks? Dancing?" Her throaty laugh was contagious. "And I bet he'd have lots of energy in bed."

Eve glanced over at the cute new waiter, took in the dark curly hair, the deep brown eyes, nice firm buns beneath his black slacks. The skin on his face was as smooth as a baby's butt. He looked over at her and winked. Eve whirled around to glare at her best friends. "He's younger than Amy."

"So is Tiffany," Tess reminded her. "So show Don by taking a younger man to the wedding."

"And buying a kick-ass dress that will make him drool," Maggie added.

"I'm really not interested in Donald's drool." But the thought of making his jaw drop with a hot dress and an even hotter date had a certain appeal.

"Hey, Mrs. Corcoran."

Eve looked up from her empty wine glass to the other new waiter working tonight. She frowned until she recognized those bright blue eyes. "Shawn? Oh my God. When did you grow up?"

He grinned. "Happened over night. I swear."

He had to be over six feet tall now, with broad shoulders Eve never remembered him having. "I hope so, because I'm suddenly feeling really old."

"Well, you don't look old. Honest, you look awesome."

Eve felt her cheeks grow warm. "Seems I remember you being a real charmer."

"Nah. It's the truth."

"Eve, aren't you going to introduce us?" Tess asked, her voice oozing her own kind of charm.

"Down girl," Maggie quipped. "He's too young, even for you."

They all laughed and Shawn winked at Tess. All men, no matter what the age, flirted with Tess. Maybe it was because Tess flirted right back. Eve had never been comfortable doing that, even back when she was Shawn's age.

"Tess Harkness and Maggie Sheridan, this is Shawn Propheter. He used to be our paperboy, I swear, like, last week."

Shawn laughed. “Pleased to meet you, ladies. I’ve just graduated from JCC, Mrs. Corcoran, so it’s been a while since I had my paper route.” He reached into the back pocket of his black trousers and pulled out an order pad. “Now I better get back to work. Can I get you ladies another drink or are you ready to order?”

They ordered another round of drinks and dinner. Eve sighed. How fast these kids were growing up. Amy was getting married. Seth had taken a job across the country. And even the younger neighborhood kids were grown. “I feel so old.”

“Nonsense,” Tess said. “We’re in our prime.” With her short stylish haircut and up to date fashions, Tess looked in her prime. Eve felt way past hers even though she was only a couple of years older.

“What happened to Jami and Rob?” Maggie asked, referring to the waitress and waiter who’d worked Wednesday nights for as long as the three of them had been meeting for dinner.

“Didn’t you hear?” Eve asked. “They eloped last week. Paid me the last month’s rent on the apartment and moved to California to try their luck in the movies.”

“No! How romantic.”

“Pretty risky, I say,” Tess added. “They’re cute kids, but do you really think they’re going to make it in Hollywood?”

“It’s possible,” Maggie said. “At least they’re giving it a shot.”

Tess was a realist, Maggie an optimist. Eve was somewhere in between. She liked to think she was balanced, but she was afraid sometimes it just made her wishy washy.

“True. No one thought a gift shop could thrive in Best Bay but it’s doing better than I ever hoped.” Eve shook her head in amazement. “One of the summer residents from Ohio came in today and ordered a full set of china for her granddaughter's wedding."

Shawn came back with their drinks. "I've got your orders in, ladies. I'll bring them out as soon as they're ready."

"Thanks, Shawn. How's everything going?"

"Great, thanks. Keeping busy." He started to turn away, then stopped. "You know, last semester I took this film course – Classic Film Making. I loved it. Part of the course we studied screen goddesses."

"They teach that at community college?" Tess asked.

Shawn laughed. "Yep."

"What do you mean, screen goddesses?" Maggie asked.

"You know, actresses like Grace Kelly and Rita Hayworth and Sophia Loren. Sexy beautiful women with class and charisma. I can't help but look at you three lovely ladies and be reminded of those screen goddesses."

"Shawn..." Eve felt her face grow warm.

"No, really. You're all classy, strong women who happen to be hot too, if you don't mind me saying so."

"I don't mind," Tess said with a wink.

He laughed again. "Well, I better get back to work. Hope I didn't embarrass you. I just couldn't resist saying that. I'll bring out your dinners as soon as they're ready."

"Wow," Tess said as they watched him walk away. "He's getting an excellent tip tonight."

"You should take Shawn to the wedding," Maggie said after she took a long drink of tea. "He's so cute and charming."

And made her feel like an old woman next to him. How could Don not feel old with a wife less than half his age? "No way. I'd feel like I was babysitting."

"No," Maggie said sharply. "You'd be showing Don

what a hot chick you are by taking a younger man to the wedding."

Eve frowned. "Just because Don's going to look like a fool doesn't mean I want to look like one."

"Good point."

"I happen to know several single men in Best Bay who aren't college age," Tess said with a grin.

"And is that *know* in the carnal sense?"

Tess shrugged and didn't even have the decency to blush. "Not all of them."

"It's just for one day," Maggie reminded her. "You're not looking for another husband. Just a good looking guy to hang on your arm." She gasped. "I know. Your neighbor."

"Who? Oh. Rick?" An image of her next door neighbor's warm brown eyes popped into her brain.

"He's hot," Maggie gushed.

"All the Best brothers are hot," Tess chimed in.

Eve agreed Rick was good looking, but... "I don't know. It seems weird. Our kids grew up together. I've always thought of him as Cathy's husband."

"But, hon," Tess said softly, "it's been a few years since she died."

"I know. It just feels weird."

"He'll understand it's just for the wedding."

"I don't know." The thought of walking up to Rick and asking him to be her wedding date was scary as hell. But then...so was the thought of walking into that church all alone. "I'll think about it."

"I think you should do it," Maggie said. "You're a sexy goddess, after all."

"Well, so are you. So how's your love life lately?"

Maggie's grin faded and Eve regretted turning the tables on her. Maggie glanced over her shoulder. "Oh, here's our food."

They waited until Shawn had served their food,

then Eve and Tess turned their attention to Maggie. "What's up, sweetie?" Tess asked.

Maggie shrugged. "I get lonely." Maggie had been a single mother since her daughter was little. Her husband had died in a motorcycle accident before he turned thirty. "I mean, I watch the grandkids for Claire a lot, but it's not the same."

"Definitely not," Tess said.

"I just don't feel like a woman anymore. I'm a mother and a grandmother and a teacher, but not just Maggie. Certainly not someone attractive to a man. I can't remember the last time I had—" Maggie stopped and looked around, then lowered her voice to a whisper. "Sex. I can't remember the last time I had sex."

Eve nodded in agreement but Tess didn't say a word, just stared into her glass.

"I guess Ms. Harkness is the only one getting any around here," Eve said. "It's been so long for me I think I've forgotten how."

"Hon, don't you know sex is like riding a bicycle?" Tess asked.

"Once you learn how you never forget?"

"There's that," Tess said with a laugh. "But I was going to say when you fall off you have to get right back on."

"That would mean I'd need someone to ride," Eve said. Maggie spit her drink across the table and Tess just grinned. Eve's face burned. "Shit. I mean someone to ride with. Um...I mean..."

"We know what you mean," Tess said, wiping off the table with her napkin. "So Rick? You probably want to ask Rick to be your wedding date before you take him for a ride."

Maggie laughed.

Eve was about to shoot back a smart remark, but paused for a moment. She'd known Rick Best for a long time. He was a good man. He'd been a good husband, father, neighbor. But if the date went badly it might make living next door to him awkward. "I don't know."

"How many other options do you have?" Maggie asked. "Well, I guess you could ask one of his brothers."

That would be even worse. "I don't know any of the others that well."

"Fine! I'll be your date." Mischief lit Tess's eyes. "We'll get the tongues wagging and no one will pay any attention to Donald and his trophy wife."

Eve laughed. "That might be fun, but you'd never be able to convince the people in this community that you've switched teams."

"Yeah," Maggie said. "You've done the deed with too many guys in town to get away with that."

Tess leaned back and sipped her drink. "Maybe I'm a good actress."

"With the way you flirt with every male still breathing? Nice try." Eve took a deep breath. "Fine. I'll ask Rick and you ask that cute young waiter."

Maggie shrieked. "You heard her!" She grabbed Eve's hand. "Call us tonight after you talk to him."

"Tonight?"

"The longer you think about it," Tess added, "the harder it will be."

Eve didn't want to admit they were right. "I just want to wait 'til the timing is perfect, you know?"

"Hon, it will never be perfect."

Chapter Two

Rick wasn't sure when he'd started keeping watch for Eve on Wednesday nights. He knew she went out with friends for dinner, came home late, usually after dark. He knew she didn't need him keeping track of her whereabouts. That went beyond the friendly-neighbor boundaries. But somehow Wednesday nights always found him sitting at his kitchen table, pouring over blueprints or the expense sheets or old photo albums, in front of the window that faced Eve's driveway.

When he saw the headlights sweep across the window as she turned into the driveway, he let out a small sigh of relief. Rick knew it was ridiculous, but he couldn't help it. He didn't have a wife to worry about anymore. His daughter was married and out of the house.

What made him think he had to worry about someone?

He stood and turned away from the window. His phone rang as he gathered up the papers and shoved them into a manila folder. He checked the caller ID before he answered. "Hey, sweetie."

"Hi, Dad. Whatcha up to?"

"Just going over a few project schedules."

"Boring."

He chuckled. He could picture his little girl, bright red hair like her mother's, curled up in a chair by the fireplace in her new house. He had to keep reminding himself that Heather wasn't a little girl any longer. She was a kindergarten teacher and the wife of a police officer now. Hard to believe. Where had the time gone?

"It's my job."

She made that little impatient huff sound that women do so well. "You shouldn't be taking work home anymore."

He shrugged, set the tea kettle on the stove and lit the burner. "It's that or watch TV. I'm not that desperate yet."

"You could go out and do something fun."

Fun? He'd forgotten how to have fun, hadn't he? "Like what?"

"Like a date."

Date? He hadn't dated in over thirty years. He wouldn't know how to date. One glance at the picture of Cathy on the wall and he knew he didn't want to. Would probably never want to again. He wasn't interested in another woman in his life.

"Dad? Dad, are you still there?"

He swallowed. "Yeah."

"It's time, don't you think?" she asked softly.

"I haven't thought about it." Didn't want to think about it.

"Come on, Dad. Mom wouldn't want you to be lonely."

He wasn't lonely. He'd gotten used to the quiet, that's all. "I know, sweetie. But..." There was a knock at the back door.

"Just promise me you'll think about it," Heather said. "Keep an open mind, okay?"

"Okay. Hold on, there's someone at the door." He opened the door to find his next-door neighbor on the back patio. It had started to rain and the humidity hung heavily in the air. "Eve. Come on in."

"Is this a bad time?"

"Not at all." He ushered her in and closed the door against rain. "Just talking to Heather."

Eve smiled, a wide, easy smile. "Tell her I said hi."

"It's Mrs. Corcoran. She says hi."

"Tell her hi for me. I just saw Amy last weekend, making plans for the bachelorette party. Hey, you know Mrs. C. and her husband broke up, don't you?"

He wasn't going there. Rick turned his back on Eve and led her into the kitchen. "You need to get your husband on a different shift so you have something better to do than bug your old man."

She laughed, her musical chuckle so much like her mother's it made his chest clench. "I'll let you go. Love ya."

"Love ya too, sweetie." He disconnected and turned sheepishly to Eve. "Sorry. You want to sit down?"

If he hadn't just had that conversation with Heather, would he have noticed how Eve's pale-green eyes sparkled? How her smooth, shoulder-length blonde hair shone against her black raincoat? She looked a little unsure and suddenly he wondered why she'd stopped by. The tea kettle whistled then. "Cathy got us into the habit of a hot cup of tea at night. I guess I've just kept it up. Would you like a cup?"

"Sure. Thanks."

He turned off the fire and took a box of lemon herbal tea bags from the cupboard. "How are you, Eve?"

"I'm okay, thanks. How're you doing?"

"Fine. How about Tess and Maggie?"

"Good. They're good."

Rick winced, his back still to Eve. Wasn't there anything they could talk about together now that the kids and spouses were gone?

"When I pulled into the driveway tonight," Eve said, "I was thinking about how busy our end of the cul-de-sac used to be. Kids coming and going all the time. It's so quiet now."

"It is." He shook his head. "And there was a time when I would have done anything for some peace and quiet."

"And now here we are," she said softly.

Here we are.

He glanced at her over his shoulder while he set the kettle back on the stove. She'd shrugged out of her coat and hung it over the back of one of the chairs. Her pale blue top clung to her slender figure. She looked every bit as good as she had twenty-five years ago. He cleared his throat when he realized he'd been checking her out. He hoped she hadn't noticed.

"Have a seat. Do you like honey?"

She was so graceful as she lowered herself into the chair. "What?"

"In your tea. Would you like a little honey?"

"That would be great."

Rick stirred a spoonful of honey into each mug and then carried them over to the table. Eve smiled her thanks and wrapped her hands around the flowered mug Cathy had always used. Rick stared at Eve's long, slender fingers, pale pink polish on the nails.

Cathy had never grown out her nails or painted them pretty colors. She'd never bothered. There'd been lots of nights when she couldn't even get all the dirt out from under her nails after working at the greenhouse all day. But damn, she'd loved to make things grow.

Rick waited for the prickle of tears to come, like they still often did when he thought about Cathy, but this time they barely prickled at all. He simply smiled at the memory.

"What are you thinking about?" Eve asked.

Fool. He'd been staring at her fingers but forgot she was there. He shook his head. "Sorry. Just one of those memories of Cathy that made me smile."

"I'm glad you can smile again."

Rick drank some tea, still drawn to Eve's fingers, the way they were now tapping absently on the side of the mug. He almost reached out and brushed the tip of his finger over a pale pink nail, but stopped before he actually broke the iron grip on his mug. "Wet out there tonight." God, could he get any less original? He'd sunk to talking about the weather.

"I know." She didn't seem to be bothered by the choice of topic. "But we can use the rain." She took another sip of her tea. "Amy said Heather's got the bachelorette party all planned."

"I don't think I want to know anything about it." Rick remembered talk of limos and wine tasting. Hell, he could still picture them as two little girls in pigtails, sitting on the family room floor with a bowl of popcorn between them, giggling at a funny movie. "But I'm glad they're still friends."

"Yeah, me too. But after a year-long engagement, it reminds me that suddenly the wedding will be here before we know it."

"How are the wedding plans coming?"

"Good. Everything's booked or ordered or reserved. I still need to buy a dress though. And I hate all the mother of the bride dresses I've seen. So dowdy looking."

"You could never look dowdy." She always looked so polished and classy.

"Thanks. But you haven't seen some of the dresses I tried on," she said lightly. She quickly looked away and stared into her tea. "But you don't want to talk about dresses." She looked up at him, down to her tea and back up again. "Um...did you get your invitation?"

"I did. I wouldn't miss it. Labor Day weekend, right?"

"End of summer. These weeks will go by so quickly."

Eve usually had everything all pulled together. He was surprised for her to seem so nervous. "Don't worry, everything will fall into place," he assured her. "It'll be a great party."

She smiled. "It will be. A night to remember."

Rick's smile faded as he was bombarded by images and emotions. "My memories of Heather's wedding are bittersweet. I like to remember what a beautiful bride she was. How happy Ryan made her. And yet the way the night ended..."

Cathy had left the reception to run home to grab some forgotten gifts for the attendants. Rick had told her not to bother, or to send someone else, but she'd blamed herself for leaving the box behind in the first place. On her way back, a drunk driver ran a stop sign and smashed into the driver's side of the car. She died before she reached the hospital.

Eve reached out and took his hand. This time the prickles came full force.

"I'm sorry. I didn't mean to bring up painful memories. Maybe I should go."

He squeezed her hand. "No. Please don't. It's nice to have someone to talk to. Even now, most people avoid talking about her with me. I like to remember her, talk about her."

"She could make anything grow."

"I'm glad Heather inherited her green thumb. This place would look like hell if she didn't come around and take care of the gardens."

"And through all those teen-age years we wondered why we ever wanted kids in the first place." Humor laced Eve's tone and Rick returned her easy smile.

"You're looking good, Eve. This past year hasn't been so easy for you."

She shrugged and then, as if she suddenly realized she was still holding his hand, she let him go and wrapped those lovely fingers around the mug again. "It's getting better every day." She said it as if she meant it, so he hoped that was true. Her eyes sparkled and made Rick grin too. Shit, he hadn't smiled this much in ages.

God, had it really been twenty-five years since they moved into this sub-division only months apart, each family with a little girl? Seth had been born a few years after, but Rick and Cathy had never been able to have any more kids. Rick remembered years of joint barbeques. Neighborhood pool parties. Kids everywhere. Cathy and Eve laughing in the back yard. Rick at the barbeque. Funny, he couldn't think of all that many times when Don had been there as the kids got older. Had he really been working all those times Eve made excuses for him?

"Don really is an ass," Rick said. The words came out a little more forceful than he'd intended.

Eve tipped her head to the side, questioning his outburst without saying a word.

"Just thinking back. Look at all he had and he never appreciated it."

She sighed and took another sip of tea. "I was angry for a long time but now, I let it go." She shrugged and grinned. "Mostly."

"I don't know how he could have let you go." Did he really say that out loud?

Eve's face turned a light pink. "Well, thank you for saying so." She set down her mug and pushed her chair away from the table. "I should be going. It's getting late." She stood up and he was already sorry to see her go.

"Did you stop over for anything particular?"

She didn't meet his eyes, focusing on buttoning her coat. "Just saw you sitting alone through the window. Wanted to say hi."

He walked her to the back door. "I'm glad you stopped by." He reached around her to open the door and caught a whiff of Eve's soft scent. She turned her head to look up at him and before he knew it, he'd brushed his lips across her smooth cheek. "Have a good night, Eve."

"You too," she whispered and hurried out into the darkness.

He rushed to the window to watch her walk across the yard and into her house. He told himself he simply wanted to make sure she got in safely, but he carried her scent with him the rest of the night.

***

Eve felt Rick's gaze on her back as she crossed the grass and hurried into the house. The rain had settled down to a gentle sprinkle. Her skin felt all shivery. She slammed the door shut and leaned back against it, her heart scrambling in her chest like a schoolgirl's. She slowly raised her hand to her cheek and smiled.

After a moment, she pushed away from the door and straightened. She didn't want to think about the last few minutes. So he'd given her a little peck on the cheek. So what? It didn't mean anything. She didn't want it to mean anything.

She'd been a coward tonight. She'd gone over there to ask Rick to be her wedding date and she'd chickened out. If she didn't do it soon, she'd find herself all alone at her daughter's wedding while her ex-husband and his young bride had a grand old time.

Her footsteps echoed on the brick-red tile floor. Tomorrow, she promised herself. She'd ask him tomorrow. Eve crossed the huge kitchen which had easily accommodated the four of them plus a large group of friends when they used to have pizza night. Don had insisted on painting the walls a dark mustard yellow that she hated. Maybe she'd paint it something bright and cheerful now.

No one had sat in the dining room in months. The large great room, with the vaulted ceiling that made it look so open, now seemed cold and ostentatious and she rarely spent time in there anymore. No more business get-togethers. No more movie nights with the kids.

Every night she climbed the long, winding staircase to the second floor which held the master suite plus four more bedrooms and two baths.

She stepped into the master suite. This was where she spent her time now when she wasn't at work. The huge bedroom had a sitting area with a sofa, chair and media center in addition to the king-sized bed she hadn't touched since Don moved out. She slept curled up on the sofa with the soft yellow throw her mother had crocheted before she died. The bathroom with the jet tub and steam shower was a luxury she wasn't ashamed to admit she enjoyed. If she had a kitchen off the other end, this would be all the space she needed.

What was she doing here in this big empty house? She didn't need this much space. Was she clinging to memories? Maybe. Some were good but some were lousy.

Amy and Seth running through the house, laughing and playing. Family dinners around the oval table in the corner of the kitchen.

Don slinking through the door, late again.

Rocking Seth to sleep. Teaching Amy to make chocolate chip cookies. Helping the kids with homework.

Don rolling away from her in bed. Confessing his

affair. Packing his bags.

Eve crossed the bedroom floor and ran her fingers over the dent in the wall. It had taken quite a while to pick all the shards of glass from the shattered vase out of the carpet.

Don had been so eager to get rid of her and their marriage that he let her have the house without any argument. But she didn't need this big house. She didn't want it.

Should she sell it?

"Hell, yeah," she shouted even though no one could hear her. With a rush of joy she realized she didn't have to talk her decision over with anyone. Didn't have to get anyone else's permission. "Ha!"

Waves of relief, of freedom, washed over her. Eve laughed out loud. She didn't have to worry about what Don or anyone else thought. She could do whatever the hell she wanted. She was an independent woman for the first time in her life and it felt damn good!

She spread her arms wide and fell back on the bed. The bed she was going to get rid of as soon as possible.

Don had gotten on with his life and it was time for her to stop pretending hers was ever going to be the same again. And now, as so many thoughts whirled around in her brain, she decided she didn't want it to be. She was ready for a new life. And to do that, she had to get away from this house.

Not giving herself time to think twice, she jumped from the bed, grabbed her cell phone and called Tess.

"You ask him yet?" Tess asked before Eve had a chance to say hello.

It took Eve a moment to realize what Tess was talking about. "No."

"Why not?"

Because I lost my nerve? "We were talking wedding plans and I thought I'd find a good opening, but then he started talking about Cathy and how she was killed at Heather's wedding reception and I just couldn't ask him."

"I can still go with you."

Eve chuckled. "No. I'll ask him." She was a strong, independent woman now. She could do whatever she wanted. "I want to sell the house."

"Are you sure?"

"It's too big for me now. It echoes."

"I can see that."

"Reminds me of everything I've lost. I don't want to dwell on the past. I want to look toward the future."

"Good for you. You want to look at smaller houses, then? You don't want to move to the city or anything?"

Eve smiled at the horror in her friend's voice. "No, don't worry. I'm going to move into the apartment." Until the words came out of her mouth, Eve hadn't realized that she was thinking about living in the now-vacant apartment above her shop.

"Is it big enough?"

Eve looked around the master suite. The apartment was bigger than this room, so what else would she need? She couldn't wait to get up there and look around. "It'll be perfect."

Chapter Three

It had been a hell of a day. Rick pulled into the driveway, tired, sweaty and more than a little irritated. His brother, Max, had called him out of the office just after lunch but that wasn't the cause of his irritation. He liked getting out to the job sites. Most days he missed it.

But why did clients have to change their minds at the last minute? Mrs. Baxter suddenly decided she had to have an island in the middle of a kitchen that wasn't designed to hold one. Now that meant the project had to be put on hold until a new kitchen design could be drawn up to fit into the same space.

And that meant they would have to order new cabinets and countertops. The homeowner would pay big time.

Why should Rick care, just because one of their crews had been wasting their time for the past week? Arguing—sorry, *discussing*—the change in plans with her all afternoon hadn't put him in the best of moods. Time to shake it off. Tonight he'd figure out where to send the guys until they could get back to the kitchen remodel.

Rick walked in the house, still overcome by the quiet that met him at the door every evening, even after all this time. He used to come home most nights to the sound of water running in the shower. Cathy used to time it just right. He headed for the bedroom, remembering all the afternoons he'd joined his wife in the shower after work. They'd scrub each other's backs and sometimes...

He sank down on the edge of the bed. He hadn't thought about Cathy so much in quite a while. Was it the conversation with Eve last night? Or was it her companionship? Her smile? Her soft scent?

Maybe Heather was right. Maybe he was ready to imagine another woman in his life.

His phone was ringing when he got out of the shower. He snagged a towel, dashed into the bedroom and grabbed the phone off the dresser.

His voice was breathless as he caught it in time. "Hello?"

"Rick? It's Eve, did I catch you at a bad time?"

"No. Just got out of the shower and I'm dripping all over the floor." His laugh cut off. Why did he tell her that? Did he *want* her to picture him naked? Did he want to *think* about her picturing him naked? Gah, he wished he'd never had that conversation with Heather.

"Sorry. Do you want to call me back when you're...um...dry...um...dressed?" Thank goodness that was amusement he heard in Eve's voice. Or was it embarrassment?

"No. Just give me a sec." Rick dropped the phone to the mattress, dried off quickly and wrapped the towel around his waist. He shook his head at his actions. Like she could see him. What was wrong with him? "Okay, I'm back. What can I do for you?"

"You know my building on Main? Where my shop is?"

"Sure." Two-story building with a brick facade. Good roof. Well-maintained from what he could see.

"I'd like to set up a time when you could come look at the apartment upstairs. It needs some work."

"I heard your tenants took off." Renters rarely treated property as well as homeowners did.

"Eloped," she corrected. "Going to try their luck in L.A. but they didn't do any damage. I just want to make a few changes before I move in. Some upgrades to the kitchen and bath. Not too much work, I hope."

"Wait a minute." He must have heard her wrong. "You're moving in? To the apartment?"

"Yes. Selling the house. Tess is bringing over the sign today, but she says she already has a couple of potential buyers so it might happen quickly."

She sounded excited, but something about not seeing Eve next door made his chest feel suddenly hollow. "Wow. You never mentioned that last night." And that was a stupid thing to say. "Sorry. I know you don't have to tell me anything. I'm just...surprised."

"Well, I only decided after I left your house last night."

"I chased you away, huh? Don't want to live next door to me anymore?" He hoped his voice sounded lighter than he felt.

"Don't be silly. But the house is way too much for just me. It needs a family, you know?"

Yeah, he knew. He'd thought the same thing a few times about this place, but he wasn't ready to leave behind the house where he and Cathy lived, where they'd raised Heather. He knew it had to have been a hard decision for Eve.

"So could you look at it and give me an estimate, or are you guys booked up a year in advance or something?"

"I can look at it. Are you free tonight?"

"Tonight? Sure. I'm still here at the apartment now."

His chest felt lighter, fuller. "I'll get dressed and be right over. Give me fifteen."

***

Eve couldn't stop thinking about the fact that Rick had been naked while she'd been talking to him. Naked. Nude. Sans clothing. All that masculine skin with nothing covering it. She blew out a shaky breath.

She'd seen him in swim trunks often enough over the years. Both of their houses had pools, and since Amy and Heather had been joined at the hip for most of their lives, and Eve and Cathy had been friends, the two families had often been at one or the other's houses.

But that was back when he'd been Cathy's husband. When she'd been Don's wife. Back then Eve had been able to appreciate a good looking man without coveting him or getting turned on. Those kinds of thoughts had never even crossed her mind.

But now...as she paced the scarred hardwood floor, Eve found herself getting all tingly at the thought of Rick having been naked while they shared words. And even more shivery knowing he was rushing over here as soon as he covered up that naked body.

What was wrong with her?

Crazy as it was, she dashed into the outdated bathroom to check her reflection in the mirror. Her hair was a mess. She shoved her fingers through the strands, trying to fluff them up a little. She'd left her purse, and the brush inside, down in her shop and she didn't have time to run down and get it now. Her lipstick was down there too. She bit her lip. Her face looked so pale when she didn't have lipstick on. At least she was still in the dress and heels she'd worn for work, so she felt as if she had at least some of her armor in place.

What was she getting so worked up about? This was

Rick. She'd known him for years. He'd seen her hundreds of times. It wasn't as if he was going to care what she looked like. He was coming to look at the apartment, not her. She should be getting her thoughts together on the work she'd like to have done, not primping in front of the mirror.

There was a knock at the door at the bottom of the stairs. "Eve?"

Rick.

Eve dashed to the stairs and then forced herself to slowly descend the steep steps. Her foolish heart was beating wildly. She seemed to have no control over it. She crossed the entryway and took a deep breath before she opened the door. "Hi. Thanks for coming right over."

Rick was one of those guys who seemed to get better looking as he got older. While he'd been long and lanky, almost skinny, when he was younger, he filled out a pair of jeans and a T-shirt real well now. The silver at his temples and threading through the rest of his hair sparkled beneath the light. And the crinkles around his brown eyes when he smiled?

There were those tingles again.

Eve realized she was just standing there, blocking his entrance. She cleared her throat and hoped the heat she felt in her face didn't stain her cheeks red. "Come on in."

He had a clipboard in one hand and began his inspection as soon as she closed the door behind him. "This is a nice-sized foyer. Is there anything you want to update in here?"

Straight to business then. She frowned and looked around her. "I hadn't thought about it."

He pointed down with the corner of the clipboard. "The floor is worn and some corners of the tiles are coming up. It wouldn't cost much to replace it with a durable vinyl that would withstand the rain and snow. A new coat of paint on the walls would brighten the space and you could get away with keeping that old ceiling fixture. It adds character but not a whole lot of light."

Eve nodded slowly, looking at the space with new eyes. He was right. "I can see you know your stuff."

The corner of his mouth quirked up. "Did you have any doubt?"

Her breath caught on a laugh. What was wrong with her? The first thought to pop into her head was, *I'd like to see your stuff.*

"Um, come on up. I think the stairs are safe and sturdy."

"Lead the way."

Rick followed her up the stairs and all she could think about was him staring at her ass. And that she liked the thought of him staring at her ass. It was as if she'd been dropped into an alternate universe.

"You'll get your exercise climbing these stairs a few times a day," he commented when they reached the top.

Eve was a little out of breath but she knew it had nothing to do with the climb. "Yeah." She looked around the landing as if seeing it for the first time. "I'm going to put a bench by the door and a coat rack there in the corner. Guess this needs some sprucing up too."

"I'd recommend the same as the foyer. New floor covering and paint the walls. The areas are small. Won't take much time or money."

"Okay." She opened the apartment door and ushered him in. He walked past her into the kitchen.

"Not a bad size," he said, "but I think we could make a better use of space. We can leave the sink where it is but if we moved the fridge here and the stove there it would be more efficient. The floor's not bad, probably just need to refinish it, but after we move things around we'll see what we run into. There's a chance we might have to replace it."

Eve bristled. She hadn't called him here to tell her how to update her apartment. "Hold on a minute."

He looked up from the clipboard where he was scribbling notes. "What?"

"Rick, I appreciate your expertise, I really do, but I wanted to talk to you about *my* plans."

"Sorry. You're right." He dropped the clipboard on the counter. "I took over, didn't I? Max usually talks to the clients who know what they want. I get called out to talk to the ones who need suggestions. Force of habit. I apologize."

"That's okay. I'm sure I'll be asking for your opinions as we go along. I realize some of my ideas may not be possible." She walked over to the empty far corner where there was a small narrow window. There was no dining room in the apartment, so this was the only place to put a table and chairs. "Let's not bother moving the appliances, it's just going to be me and I'm not worried so much about efficiency. Just refinish the floor. What I'd really love is a bigger window here. As big as you can make it. I want more light and to be able to see the garden out back while I eat."

Rick joined her at the window. It looked down on the community garden that had grown up on the vacant lot on the other side of the rear alley. Cathy and a few of her friends from the greenhouse had started it a few years before, and it had flourished since then. Vibrant flowers shared space with small vegetable and herb plots.

"How about a bay window?" he asked.

"Really? With a little sill?" She loved that idea.

"Sure. Or if you aren't hung up on privacy we could make this entire section of wall window, from floor to ceiling. It would give you a lot more light, and you'd have a great view. But of course, then you'd want to get dressed for breakfast, if you usually eat in your nightgown." He groaned. "Sorry. I don't know why I said anything about your nightgown."

"I don't wear a nightgown." The words were out of Eve's mouth before she could stop them.

Rick's gaze shot up from the clipboard. The heat in his gaze was palpable. His Adam's apple bobbed as he swallowed. "So that's a no for the window wall?"

"Oh, I want it." Was he as affected by her as she was by him? She couldn't stop the grin. "I have a robe."

"Right." He cleared his throat and made some more notes on his clipboard. "If there's nothing else in the kitchen, let's take a look at the bath."

"Sounds good." She led him into the bathroom and once they were both in the small space, she shut the door, thinking it would be better for him to see the whole room at once.

But when she turned around, there was Rick, standing so close she could feel the heat of his body. So close she could catch his clean, masculine scent. She could see the lashes framing his eyes. Eyes that were focused on her, not on the old cast iron bathtub or the pink ceramic wall tiles.

Eve cleared her throat and tore her gaze away from him. She'd been surprised by the sudden attraction. At first it was cool and pretty amazing, because after Don she wasn't sure if she'd ever feel this way again. But the timing couldn't be worse. She was finally free, she didn't need to get mixed up with feelings for another man. Even a nice guy like Rick.

Back to business.

"So I know this room is old and tacky. The pink tiles were here when I bought the building. They were okay for tenants, but I don't want to live with them. I know it will probably be a big pain to pull them out but I hate them. And I want a vanity with a counter top and storage instead of this pedestal sink." She took a breath and went on. "And do you think there is any possible way we could make room for a steam shower in here?" It was one thing she would miss from her house.

Rick had backed up to the opposite wall while she'd babbled, as far away from her as he could get in the space. He was writing again. Of course he was, that's what he was here for.

A bigger bathroom would have been nice, but this was what she had to work with if she wanted to live here. And she did. It would be worth it. Her own apartment. Her own space. She didn't have to share it with anyone. She didn't have to ask anyone if it was okay to knock out part of a wall to put in a window or to get rid of the perfectly good tile. Or to question if she really needed a steam shower.

Rick was quiet for so long that she wondered if *he* was going to ask her if she really needed an extravagant shower or to chastise her for wanting to get rid of perfectly good Pepto-pink tiles. "First of all, we don't have to pull down the tiles. We can paint them."

"Really? I had no idea. That would be great."

He pointed to the opposite end of the room. "What's on the other side of this wall?"

She had to think a moment. "Combination coat closet and pantry."

"Would you be willing to give up the closet for your shower?"

Her breath caught. Just like that he'd found solutions for her problems. No sneer that said he didn't think she should be asking for something so frivolous. No attempt to talk her out of any of her suggestions.

When she couldn't find the words to tell him how much that meant to her, he must have thought she didn't think the sacrifice would be worth it. "What if I can find you other pantry storage in the kitchen and build you a small coat closet at the end of the landing?"

"You could do that?" Tears prickled her eyes.

He grinned and pulled a tape measure out of his pocket. "Let's find out."

She followed him out onto the landing and he showed her where he could turn some wasted space into an area for coats and boots. Then he studied the pantry closet, took measurements and assured her it would give her enough space for the steam shower and he would still have room to build in narrow shelves floor to ceiling for storage of her cans and boxes.

Eve wanted to throw her arms around him in gratitude but if she did, she'd probably never let him go.

She showed him the cozy living room. He walked around, studying the windows, walls, ceiling, floor. She found herself studying him and then forcing herself to stop studying him. "I had the room painted this soft gray before Rob and Jami moved in. I'm going to keep it."

"The hardwood floors look in good shape too," Rick said.

"They were good tenants."

"Anything need to be done in the bedroom?" His voice sounded nonchalant, but the rumble touched something deep inside her.

She was overwhelmed. He overwhelmed her.

"No. No, I don't think so." But she opened the door and led him into the room. It was a good size, plenty of room for the new bed she planned to buy. She didn't mind the high windows in this room. They gave her light while still affording her the privacy she needed in here.

Rick seemed to give the room only a cursory glance, then headed straight for the closet. He opened the door, then looked back at her with a raised brow. "And this is okay for you?"

It was just one big space, barely a walk-in with rods down each side. She shrugged. "The other things are more important to me."

"Eve, this is an easy fix. Max is a genius at storage and organization. We have customers calling just to have him design closets and pantries and garage storage. Why don't I give him the dimensions and have him draw you up a couple of options?"

"Okay." She watched him take the measurements. "I guess you do need to tell me what I want."

He turned and caught her gaze. Was he thinking about her sleeping here in the nude? Or thinking about telling her what she wanted? Here? In the bedroom?

This was Rick. When had he become a man who could make her tingle? A man who could make her *want*.

No.

She didn't *want* to want him.

But she couldn't look away from either.

He cleared his throat. "What can I say? I know my stuff."

Damn but she still wanted to see his stuff.

Just then she heard the door slam and someone stomping up the stairs.

"Mom!" It was Amy. Eve recognized that I'm-not-happy tone of her voice.

Eve tore her gaze from Rick's, glanced at the door, then flicked her eyes back to him for a quick moment before leaving the bedroom.

Her daughter flew into the apartment. She'd always done everything at light-speed.

"What's the matter?" Eve asked.

"How can you ask that?" Amy's hands fluttered as she spoke. "I came by the house to see you, and Tess was pounding a For Sale sign in the front yard! How could you sell our house? And not even talk to me about it?"

Maybe Eve did still have someone she needed to talk with before she made life altering decisions.

No. This was her life now.

"Sweetie, both our lives have changed dramatically. You're getting married. You have a whole new life ahead of you. You've already moved in with Blake and I don't recall that you consulted me about that."

"No, but—"

"I'm no longer married. I have a new life ahead of me too. And I don't want to live alone in that big house that reminds me of my old life."

"Was your old life so bad?"

"Oh, no, sweetie. But it's not my life anymore."

Amy swept her gaze around the kitchen. "So you're really going to live here?"

"I am. It's the perfect size for me and I can't beat the commute."

"It just...doesn't look like you."

"It will when I'm done." The excitement was welling up inside her, ready to burst. "Mr. Best is helping me with some ideas for updates. It'll be a while before the house sells, I'm sure, so I'll have time. But that reminds me. You have to get all your stuff out of there as soon as you can." Both of the kids' bedrooms looked the same as when they moved out.

"But I'm so busy with all the wedding plans. Can't it wait until after the wedding?" Before Eve could reply, Amy propped her hands on her hips. "And what about Seth's crap? Are you going to make him fly back here to clean his stuff out?"

Eve realized she hadn't really thought all of this through yet. "We'll think of something. Just remember you need to get everything you want to keep out of there before I have a sale."

"A sale?"

"I'll call Sally McBride. She'll take care of everything. I'm getting all new furniture for this place."

"Don't you think you're going a little bit overboard?"

"Not at all." She was never again going to sleep in that king bed she'd shared with Don. She couldn't shake the feeling he shared it with Tiffany too. "None of the furniture would fit in here anyway."

"I guess you're right." Amy looked over Eve's shoulder. "Oh, hi, Mr. Best, I didn't know you were here."

"Hi, Amy." He joined them in the center of the kitchen, his clipboard in hand. "I just need to take a few more measurements and then I'll be out of here. I should have some ideas to go over with you in the next day or two, Eve, and then I can work up an estimate."

"I have to be leaving anyway," Amy said quickly. "It's my turn to cook and Blake has a massive appetite." She kissed Eve on the cheek, waved to Rick, and was gone.

"Hurricane Amy," Rick said with a smile.

"Blows in, stirs things up, and then blows out again."

"She was just surprised." Rick took a few more measurements.

"I know. I was going to call her after dinner but we got a little busy here."

"Speaking of dinner, I don't have as massive an appetite as Blake, but I am hungry. I assume you haven't eaten yet." He shoved the tape measure in his pocket and shot her a grin. That deadly grin. "Want to head over to the BB&G? We can talk some more about your plans while we eat."

Eve knew it was a bad idea to let those tingles lead the way, but she locked up the apartment, grabbed her purse from the office in the back of her gift shop, and went to dinner with Rick Best.

Chapter Four

The Best Bar and Grill was a quick walk down Main from Eve's building. Rick had never understood how women could walk in those high-heeled shoes, but as they walked together down the sidewalk, he couldn't help but appreciate how fantastic they made Eve's long legs look. She wore a classy yellow dress that skimmed her body and matched the color of her strappy sandals. His hand kept wanting to reach out and take hers as they strolled down the block.

The BB&G was owned by Rick's cousin Jimmy. He waved from behind the bar as Rick and Eve headed for the dining room. "Hey, Ricky!" Jimmy called out. "Two drafts?"

Rick sent him a thumbs-up after Eve nodded, then led her over to a small table in the middle of the dining room. The place was a comfortable mix of homespun diner and sports bar. Sports memorabilia and photographs of local sights shared space on the dark-stained shiplap walls. He shoved the clipboard under his chair and grabbed the menu. Not that he needed it.

He'd felt like an eavesdropper back at Eve's apartment. He could understand Amy's confusion and surprise, though. Eve had moved quickly with big changes. But then, her marriage had been over for a while and those thoughts of change might have been hanging around the fringes of her mind since then.

"Hey, guys." Diane, a long-time waitress, set the chilled mugs in front of them. Her curious gaze bounced back and forth between him and Eve. "You know what you want?" she asked. They ordered the BB&G's signature burgers and fries to go with the beer.

Anyone who didn't know Eve would take one look at the elegant persona and assume she only ate lobster and drank champagne. But Eve had sat at a picnic table in their back yard plenty of times. Had downed pitchers of beer with the best of them and polished off burgers and ribs and hot dogs.

He loved how many layers she had. Only her friends knew that the classy woman who sold expensive china and crystal, silver candlesticks and elegant stationary, loved to shop yard sales and flea markets. That the woman who enjoyed entertaining the upper crust when her husband wanted to network, was just as happy cooking marshmallows in the living room fireplace to make s'mores.

But even her friends might be surprised to know that after living in a five-bedroom, four-bath home with landscaped grounds, Eve would be happy moving to a one-bedroom walk-up above her business in the heart of the village.

Of course, she still wanted her steam shower. Rick chuckled at her excitement when he told her he could make it work.

Eve looked up from the menu. "What?"

"Nothing. Sorry. Just thinking about the changes you asked for."

"Not what you expected?"

He shrugged. "You knew what you wanted. Most people don't."

"Do you know this apartment will be the first place I've lived on my own? Ever. In my whole life."

"Really?"

"I moved from home where my dad ruled with an iron fist to a college dormitory with roommates and then married Don as soon as I graduated." She flashed Rick a cocky grin. It was sexy as hell. "I'm independent for the first time in my life. So yeah, I'm going to ask for what I want this time."

"Nothing wrong with that."

She nodded and glanced around the dining room. Most of the tables were occupied and more than a few pairs of eyes were trained on them. There was an awkward tension in the air between them and Rick realized he should have thought twice about inviting her to eat in a busy restaurant filled with nosy neighbors.

"The rumors will be starting," she murmured.

He shrugged, surprised he didn't care. "I could pick up my clipboard and wave it in the air. We could talk about windows and showers at the top of our lungs."

She laughed. "Not necessary." She dropped her voice. "Um...I've been wanting to ask you something and now's as good a time as any."

"That sounds serious."

"No. Awkward. Embarrassing."

She'd made him curious, but at least she hadn't lost her smile. "Okay? What is it?"

Eve took a deep breath. "The wedding. Amy's wedding. Do you have a date? Because I don't. And Don's going to be there with his cute young wife and—"

She broke off as the door to the restaurant opened and a familiar booming laugh proceeded a fifty-something lawyer and his new twenty-something wife into the place. Eve's eyes met Rick's and her hand tightened on her beer mug. Speak of the devil. And of course, Don Corcoran headed straight for their table as soon as he spotted them.

"And I was having such a good time," Eve murmured. Seeing her ex-husband made her lose the smile and that pissed off Rick more than anything.

He plastered a big grin on his face and grabbed her hand as Don and Tiffany approached. Eve's eyes widened, but she didn't say a word. When her ex stopped at their table, Rick looked up, acting surprised. "Oh, hi, Don. How are you?"

Don frowned as his eyes bounced from Eve's face to her hand in Rick's. "I never pictured you two as a couple." His voice was one of those that carried across a crowded room. Probably good for a lawyer in a courtroom, not so good for a jerk in the middle of a restaurant.

Rick shrugged. "Probably some people thought the same about you and Tiff."

Don's expression darkened. Tiffany hung back, her hands twisting the strap of her tiny pink purse.

"Did you want something, Don?" Eve asked.

"We need to talk about the wedding." As if it was obvious.

"Amy's wedding?"

"Of course, Amy's wedding." Don narrowed his eyes. "Is there another wedding I don't know about?"

Eve's mouth quirked. She glanced at Rick before she looked back at her ex-husband. "What do we need to talk about?"

"Things," Donald said dryly.

"Okay, but not now, for heaven's sake. Call me later and I'll see when I can fit you in."

Rick felt her trembling. He squeezed her hand. Diane was heading their way. "Here's our food."

Tiffany's eyes bounced back and forth between them. Her expression looked almost apologetic.

"Donny, I'm hungry. Let's get a table."

Diane came up with a plate in each hand. "There's a table free over there by the wall," she told Tiffany, nodding to the other side of the room. "We're filling up fast. You might want to grab it."

Don huffed. "I'll talk to you later," he said to Eve. He turned away when Tiffany tugged at his arm.

"Good to see you," Rick tossed off.

He watched them cross the room, then looked up at Diane. "Thanks."

Diane smiled as she set down the plates in front of them. "You need anything else?"

Eve shook her head. "Thanks."

"You guys look good together," Diane said with a wink. Her silver ponytail bounced as she nodded.

"Oh, we're not—"

Rick cut Eve off by lifting their still-entwined hands and kissing her knuckles. "Thanks, Di, but this is all still very new. We didn't expect to get all this attention."

She rolled her eyes as if to say he should have known better. "Let me know if you need anything."

Eve tugged her hand free. "Why did you let her think we're a couple?"

"Eve, everyone in here thinks we're a couple now. Especially after Don announced it to the world. And you didn't tell him any different."

"I know." She doused her fries with ketchup and vinegar. "What are we going to do now?"

"Nothing unless you want to. I did get the impression you wanted me to ask you to be my date for Amy's wedding, though."

And there was that smile again. "I thought I asked you to be *my* date."

"That worked out then, didn't it?" Rick hadn't expected that rush of...pleasure?...when he thought about it.

"Yeah. I guess."

"So we'll just play it casually until the wedding. It's only a few weeks away, right?" Rick hadn't realized until now how much he liked the idea of dating Eve. "Then afterward we can say we broke up, if that's what you want."

"Of course, we'll have to break up. We're not really together." Her voice had dropped to a loud whisper. "I just got my independence for the first time in my life, Rick. I'm not going to get wrapped up with another guy."

Rick signaled to Diane to bring him another beer. Maybe he should have gone for the whiskey. "Glad to know I'm just another guy to you."

"That didn't come out right, but you know what I mean. This isn't a real date. We're not really a couple."

He downed the rest of his first beer. "Pity."

***

Pity? Eve couldn't believe Rick said that. Did that mean he really wanted them to be a couple? Not just a pretend couple? He'd never said anything like that before. What was he playing at? Her head hurt just thinking about it.

"I'm too old for games, Rick," she sighed.

"This isn't a game." He put his hand on hers again and she couldn't bring herself to pull away. "I like you, Eve. I don't have anything against us being seen together. It's going to be easier than trying to deny our relationship to everyone who's already seen us here together, and everyone who will hear about it. Let's just play along until the wedding."

"Play? Sounds like a game to me."

"Not if we know the rules."

"And what are the rules?"

"What do you want the rules to be? I've already said I don't mind us being seen together. In fact, the longer

I'm with you, the more certain I am that I'd honestly like to see if something could develop between us."

"Oh, Rick..." Not now. Not when she was finally in control of her life. "That's not a good idea."

He kissed her hand again. "Careful. You don't want Donald to think we've broken up already."

The first time his lips touched her hand, Don had been standing there glaring at her and she really hadn't been able to focus and savor the feeling. But this time when Rick's warm lips brushed over the back of her hand, she felt more than tingles. Shivers shimmered over her body.

She glanced across the room and saw Donald looking their way. What would it hurt to let him think she and Rick were a couple? She'd wanted him to see her with a date at the wedding anyway. It could be even more fun to flaunt the fact that even though he'd discarded her, she'd found a hot new guy who wanted her.

She leaned across the table until they were nearly close enough for her lips to meet Rick's. "So we hang out together from time to time?"

"Right."

"We hold hands and maybe engage in other public displays of affection?"

"I think it only makes sense."

"What about in private?" Where had that come from?

He lifted a brow. "There are some things we'd only want to do in private."

Her body came alive with his words, even though she wished it wouldn't. Images followed. Rick's arms around her. His hands on her. His lips on her too. Lying in bed with him. Making love with him. No! This wasn't the place. "Oh, Rick..."

He winked. "Like paint your foyer and refinish your

floors."

She chuckled in relief but she quickly realized it wasn't relief at all. It was more like disappointment. But that was the way it had to be. She wanted to hold onto her pride long enough for Don to think a handsome nice guy like Rick wanted to spend time with her. She wanted a date for her daughter's wedding.

But even more she wanted to grasp onto her newly found independence and not let go.

***

Rick sat back in his chair before he leaned in those last few inches and caught Eve's mouth with his. He planned on kissing her soon, but he didn't want the first time to be in the middle of a crowded dining room with her ex-husband looking on.

He turned his concentration back to finishing his burger and then Eve did the same. The conversation seemed to have died out as they ate. Maybe he was kidding himself. Maybe they didn't have anything to talk about besides the apartment renovations. Maybe Heather's prompting had sent him in the wrong direction.

But no, there was something there. Little sparks of attraction. Snappy banter and hot glances. Enough to be worth a try at a relationship. And another attempt at conversation. He didn't want things to become silent and stilted between them.

He looked up from his plate. "Any other questions or ideas on the renovations before I write up the estimate?"

"Not that I can think of right now. How far out are you booked? I'll want to move in as soon as you're done."

"Actually we had to put a job on hold because the client decided to make some changes to her original kitchen design. I could have a crew out tomorrow to start, but you'll want to see the estimate first."

"Rick, I want your company to do the work. I trust you to charge me a fair price and if you can get started that quickly, that would be awesome. Get the estimate to me as soon as you can so I know what we're talking about, but yes, please. Start."

"Okay."

"He's still watching us." Eve shifted her gaze to the other side of the dining room. "Starting to piss me off."

"Forget about him."

"Wish I could. I wonder what he wants to talk about."

Rick reached across the table and gently stroked a finger down her cheek. "Forget about him."

She blinked. "Forget about who?"

He chuckled. He'd finished his burger and stole some leftover fries off Eve's plate. "Do you want another beer?"

"No. Thanks. I'm good." She crumpled up her napkin. "I probably should get going."

"In a rush to get home?"

"Not really. You?"

"Nothing to rush home to."

"Yeah. But now I have to start sorting through stuff...you know...twenty-five years' worth of stuff. What do I keep? What do I toss? What do I sell? What do I do with the stuff I want to keep but don't have room for? What do I do with the kids' stuff? Can I make a bonfire out of any of Don's crap he left behind?"

Rick laughed. "I can lend you some matches."

"I'll let you know if I run out."

He gestured to Diane for the bill. After he took care of it, he said, "I'll walk you to your car."

Eve looked like she might have been going to argue, but she just said, "Thanks."

Rick told himself it was for Donald's benefit that he

took Eve's hand in his before they walked out the door. The July evening was warm with only a hint of the mugginess that usually plagued the summer air. There were a few other people walking the sidewalk in the center of Best Bay. Lucy Lake was visible at the end of Main, where the street ended at the lake park. They didn't walk that far, but turned at the corner to hit the back alley where the parking places for the shops and apartments were, leaving the street parking for customers.

He liked the feel of her hand in his. He'd been surprised that she hadn't tugged free of his grasp before now. But as soon as her car came into view, she did just that.

"Thanks for walking me."

"Happy to."

"I'm excited to get the apartment ready."

"We'll give you some options. Colors. Floor coverings. Style of window. Features in the steam shower. Configurations in the closet. Prices. You'll make the final decision on everything. We won't order anything until you give us the okay."

"Sounds good."

"You won't miss the house?" *You won't miss me?*

She shook her head. "Like I told Amy. That's not my life anymore."

Rick stepped up close. He wanted to be a part of her new life. He reached out and swept a strand of hair away from her face. His gaze locked with hers. "You have another decision to make. Right now."

"What's that?" Her voice was a little breathless.

He slid his hand along her jaw. "Will you let me kiss you?"

Her tiny gasp made him think of hot nights in dark rooms. "You want to kiss me?"

"Right now, more than anything."

Her tongue darted out and wet her lips. "Well, I did agree to PDAs."

"Yes, you did."

"And we probably should get the first kiss out of the way so that if we need to do it in front of other people, it wouldn't look awkward."

"Eve?"

"Yes?"

"You're overthinking this."

"I know."

"Don't be nervous." He leaned in. "May I kiss you?"

"Okay," she whispered.

Rick leaned in the rest of the way, first brushing his lips along hers in a tentative, testing taste. So sweet. She was so sweet. He took a deep breath, drawing in her scent. It sent a punch to his belly and a powerful craving he didn't expect. Wrapping an arm around her waist, he drew her up against him. Her hands flew to his shoulders. He captured her lips then with a passion he hadn't felt in a very long time.

She opened for him and he delved in for a deeper kiss. He stroked her tongue with his, stoking the sudden blaze. She wriggled against him and then whimpered before sucking on his tongue. Holy hell, she heated him down to his bones.

When they separated, they were both breathing hard. Her expression told him she was as surprised as he was by the intensity of a simple kiss.

"I don't know if we should do that again." Eve backed up only a step before bumping up against the hood of her car.

"I think we should. And often."

"Rick..." There was a flash that might have been fear in her eyes, but he was sure she wasn't afraid of him. She was afraid of what she felt in that kiss.

"Okay. No more kissing today." He stepped back.

Didn't want her to feel as if he was crowding her.

She cleared her throat and opened the driver's door. "Well, I have to get home."

"Stuff to go through."

"Right."

"Okay, I'll call you as soon as we have the estimate drawn up." As if this was the end of a normal business meeting. "Good night, Eve." He turned away when all he wanted was to pull her into his arms again. This was crazy.

"Oh wait," Eve called out. "Are you really going to have a crew start in the morning?"

"Sure." He had a bunch of phone calls to make when he got back to his truck. A crew to schedule for demo and prep. And looking at his empty hands, he realized he was going to have to go back to the BB&G to grab his clipboard.

She dug in her purse. "I'll give you a spare key. In case they want to get started before I get to the shop."

"Good." He took the key, managing to take it without purposely brushing his fingers against hers. "Talk to you tomorrow."

He strode from the alley without looking back. He knew how important her independence was to Eve. Apparently no one had let her make very many of her own decisions in the past. He didn't want to stop her from having control over her life. She had to make her own choices.

Still, Rick hoped like hell that in the next two months he would be able to convince Eve to choose him over a life alone.

Chapter Five

"Hey Ricky! Did you forget something?" Jimmy called to Rick as soon as he stepped back through the door of the BB&G. "Diane found this under your chair." He reached under the bar, pulled out the forgotten clipboard, and handed it to Rick with a smile. "Mind was on something else when you left, huh?"

"Thanks." All his notes for Eve's job were on that clipboard. Rick turned to leave, then he paused when he heard familiar laughter ring out from farther down the bar. His brothers must have gotten here while he was out back kissing Eve.

"It's got to be a woman that makes a man forget all about work." Max grinned at him from beneath his bushy white mustache. "I thought that clipboard was permanently attached to your hand."

"She got you wrapped around her finger already?" John laughed in that rumbling voice he had. Rick had never figured out how the youngest and smallest of the Best brothers got the deepest voice. "Too busy to have a drink with us?"

Rick shook his head, then grabbed a stool beside his brothers. "Coffee for me, Jim. I have a lot of *work* to do when I get home."

"Nice try at deflecting," Max said. "Jimmy told us all about you and Eve Corcoran getting cozy at one of the tables and then walking out of here together holding hands."

Hell. He hadn't thought about word about him and Eve getting out to the rest of his family. At least not yet.

"Didn't you just hit the big 5-0?" Rick nudged Max's muscular arm with his elbow. "Thought you would have grown up by now."

"Dontcha know he's never going to grow up?" John was the baby Best brother. He'd only just hit the not-as-big 4-0. But he was an expert electrician.

"Mom's going to be thrilled," Max went on. "She's been hoping you'd find someone to help you get over Cathy."

Rick froze. "Cathy is not someone to *get over*," he ground out. He'd never forget Cathy. Never stop loving her. Never stop grieving the life they could have had together.

"Man." Max winced. "I'm sorry. That's not what I meant. You know that. Just that you were smiling like a fool when you walked in just now, and I haven't seen you smile like that in ages. I'm happy for you."

A twinge of guilt speared Rick's chest. Maybe it wasn't a good idea to try for a relationship with Eve after all. Not a real one. He *didn't* want to get over Cathy. And that wouldn't be fair to Eve.

Time to change the subject. "Listen, I got us a job to fill in the time til the Baxter kitchen is ready to go again. Eve is moving into the apartment above her shop and is hiring us to do a few upgrades." He explained about the floors and walls, the window and the closet, and the steam shower she had her heart set on. They were deep in conversation when Max raised a brow just before Rick felt a tap on his shoulder. He turned on the stool to see Don Corcoran standing there, his expression stormy.

"Hey, Don."

Apparently, Rick's friendly tone of voice didn't help things. Don seemed to loom menacingly over him. "What are you doing with Eve, Best?"

"Making her a hell of a lot happier than you ever did." The words flew out of his mouth before he even thought about it.

"Fuck you!" Don grabbed Rick's shoulder and dragged him from the barstool. Rick stumbled out of his grip. Max and John jumped up to have his back. Don's hands were curled into fists. Was this seriously going to happen?

"Bar fight? Is that what you really want?" Rick was aching to strike Eve's cheating ex, but he knew it wouldn't be a good idea. First of all, he'd never fought anyone but his brothers and that had been a hell of a long time ago. Secondly, he had a feeling Eve wouldn't be all that happy about it if he took a swing at Don. And last, he knew Jimmy wouldn't be thrilled if they caused any damage to his place.

But he wasn't going to back away.

Tiffany grabbed Don's arm. "Come on. I'll drive you home." Don let her tug him away, but threw a glare at Rick before he stormed out. The young woman met Rick's eye. "Sorry. Too many manhattans." Then she followed her husband out of the bar.

"What the hell?" Rick looked down at his hands, realizing they were clenched into fists as well. He turned to stare at his brothers as he stretched his fingers. His heart raced with leftover adrenaline.

"What a dick. Too bad you didn't get a punch in." John pantomimed as if he'd wanted to get a one-two punch in himself.

“No, Rick wouldn’t want to hurt his hands,” Max said as they got back on their stools. “Not only would he not be able to do his paperwork, he wouldn’t be able to hold that pretty lady of his.”

“Yeah, but she could kiss it and make it all better,” John said like the idiot little brother he’d always been.

Rick ignored them and nodded to Jimmy for a refill, wishing it was the hard stuff instead of caffeine. “I don’t remember Don being the violent type.” The lawyer had never come across to Rick as the physically threatening jerk, more like the condescending intellectual asshole. Had Donald ever hit Eve? No, there’d been nothing to indicate that in all the years they’d know each other but the thought made Rick’s blood boil.

“We should have noticed how much he’d been drinking.” Jimmy filled his coffee cup. “People do stupid things when they’ve had too much to drink.”

“Does Don get drunk in here often?”

Jimmy shook his head. “If you ask me, it was all because he saw Eve here with you. Probably one of those guys who even if they don’t want a woman, don’t want anyone else to have her either. It’ll blow over.”

“I hope so.” Rick didn’t want to worry about Eve. He turned back to his brothers. Back to work. He tapped his finger on the clipboard on the bar in front of him. “Anything else we need to cover before the morning?”

They both shook their heads. Max finished his beer and John threw back the rest of his bourbon. Rick stared into his coffee cup after they’d left. What a crazy evening.

He knew the glib words he’d thrown at Don had truth in them. Rick could tell Eve had been happy with him tonight, even when she thought she shouldn’t be. And damn if she didn’t make him happy too. And that kiss had been off the charts. Heather had given her blessing, in fact, her nudge was what had started this whole thing.

Cathy wouldn't want him to be lonely. He rubbed his chest. The pang of guilt he'd felt before eased. Cathy would never have been one of those people who if she couldn't have him, wouldn't want anyone else to have him either.

He hopped off the stool and waved to Jimmy. Time to get home and make some plans. And tomorrow night he got to see Eve again.

***

The next evening, Eve sat cross-legged on the floor in front of the upstairs hallway closet, awash with memories. She'd forgotten about the shoebox full of photos tucked away on the top shelf. If she ever found the time, she'd have to get them organized. Maybe into photo albums? Or maybe she should scan them onto the computer? She laughed to herself. They'd probably never leave this box. And that was okay because she was taking it with her.

Amy and Seth had loved goofing it up for the camera ever since they were little. Eve shuffled through the photos. Birthdays. Vacations. Graduations.

Tears prickled her eyes. Where had the time gone?

She'd made sure she gave her kids the kind of family life she'd never had. Her father had refused to take trips or go on vacations. He thought they were a waste of time and money. And what Dad wanted was all that mattered. Her mother would never cause any trouble, so Eve had learned not to as well.

Eve paused at a photo from Disney World, one of the few vacation destinations Seth and Amy had agreed on. Eve and Don had grudgingly waited in long lines and spent too much money on souvenirs, just to make their kids happy.

The doorbell rang. She shoved the box to the side and jumped to her feet. She'd had a busy day at the shop, so she'd missed Rick's call that morning. He'd left a message that he would stop over tonight with the remodeling contract for her to go over. She smoothed her hair and brushed the dust off her shorts. Her blood rushed as she dashed down the stairs.

She couldn't deny she was looking forward to seeing Rick again. Thoughts of that kiss had kept her up last night. His taste. The press of his lips on hers. The way he'd pulled her close. Would he kiss her again tonight? Should she kiss him first? She definitely wanted another kiss.

Even if she shouldn't.

Eve yanked the door open but it wasn't Rick standing on the front steps. Would there ever be a time when seeing her ex-husband didn't put her back up?

Don pushed by her into the foyer and then turned on her. "What's that For Sale sign doing in the front yard?"

She didn't even resist the urge to roll her eyes. "I thought that would be obvious."

"You're selling? After you wanted the damn house so bad?"

Eve shrugged. She almost told him about the new independent life she'd discovered and the apartment that would be her home and no one else's, but he'd probably just give her that condescending sneer. She almost said simply that this was too much house for her now, but she realized she didn't owe him any explanations at all. So she didn't say anything.

"You changed the lock," he complained after a moment of silence.

"Of course, I changed the lock," she snapped. "You never gave me back your key."

"What? You thought I was going to steal something?"

"You have no right to simply walk in here anymore. So I changed the lock."

Don shook his head as if she worried about stupid things. "We need to talk."

"You were supposed to call first. I'm busy."

"What's the matter with you? You never used to be so hardheaded and stubborn."

She shrugged again. She thought she'd married a man completely different from her father. Polished instead of crude. Well-spoken instead of coarse. But they'd both been controlling men in their own ways. She'd been so used to giving in. To *not* rocking the boat, that she'd never realized it until she was finally on her own.

When she didn't say anything else, he cleared his throat. "Well, I'm here now so let's get this done."

"What are you so angry about?" she asked. He was the one who broke up the marriage, the one who cheated, the one who moved out.

"I'm not angry. Upset." He took a deep breath and gave her that I'm-trying-to-be-patient look. "I'm worried about you."

She crossed her arms. "You don't deserve to be worried about me anymore."

"I still care about you, Eve."

"Really?" She hated arguing with him. He always seemed to bring her down to his level, getting little digs in, making her annoyed. "Is that what you want to talk about? You're worried about me?"

"No. I wanted to talk—" He frowned and looked around the foyer as if he was seeing it for the first time. "Can we sit down?"

She wanted to be petty and say no, but she nodded toward the living room. Don strode through the wide doorway.

The doorbell rang again. Probably Rick. This was going to be interesting.

Eve opened the door to her next door neighbor and wanted to sigh he looked so good. The warm summer breeze had tousled his hair and his arms and legs were tanned beneath the white T-shirt and khaki shorts. His smile warmed her heart. All the negativity that Don had brought in blew out the open door. Rick made her happy. She was in deep trouble because at the moment she couldn't seem to care.

"Hi. Come on in."

Rick carried a worn leather case. He'd said he had some flooring samples for her to look at too, as well as paint colors and window styles. And shower and closet options. Excitement buzzed through her. She couldn't wait.

"What are you doing here?"

Eve glanced over her shoulder to see Don had come back into the foyer. Oh yeah. How quickly she forgot. They had to *talk*.

"I invited him over," she told her ex with some satisfaction. She leaned over and gave Rick a quick kiss. His eyes flashed with amusement. She took his hand. "Come on. We're in here."

Don frowned. "But we need to talk, Eve."

"I know. Is it anything so personal that you don't want Rick to hear?" She took the sofa and pulled Rick down beside her. She hated that Don made her feel so juvenile, but she couldn't help it.

Frowning seemed to be Don's new expression. She remembered when he used to have a smile whenever he looked at her. When had he stopped smiling at her? How long had he been unhappy?

But as she reveled in the relief she felt for not being married to Donald any longer, Eve wondered how long she'd been unhappy and hadn't even realized it.

Don took the chair he'd always sat in, the one the kids had called the Dad Chair. Don looked from Eve to Rick and back, then sighed. "Wedding seating," he said. "We want to get it straightened out so it doesn't become awkward."

We as in Don and Tiffany? "Wedding seating is up to Amy."

"She wants us to sit at the same table, the parents' table she called it. But she wants us to work it out so there are no problems on her wedding day." He had his I'm-a-lawyer-but-I-can-speak-down-to your-level tone of voice going. Eve hated that tone.

Amy had never told her she was worried about her parents getting along at her wedding. "*I* won't cause any problems." Eve raised her brows. "Will you?"

"Of course not."

"Then we have nothing to worry about. I want Amy's wedding day to be as perfect as it can be and I won't do anything to spoil it."

"Good. There are six chairs at each table. Me and Tiffany and you make three. So my dad and Tiffany's parents can fill out the table."

Eve's parents were both deceased and Don's mother had passed away last spring. But that table seating Don had so smugly arranged wasn't going to work.

"No. Rick's my date. He sits at the table with me."

"He's not Amy's parent."

"Neither is Tiffany."

"She's my wife."

"He's my boyfriend."

Eve thought she heard Rick make a strangled noise. She realized she was holding his hand really hard so she lightened her grasp.

"I have a better idea," Eve said. "Blake's parents should have the other two seats. Or did you forget about the groom? Marie and George belong at the parents' table."

Don cleared his throat, then nodded. "You're absolutely right. Sometimes I worry so much about how Tiffany will fit into our family that I go a little overboard."

Eve wanted to scream that Tiffany would never *fit*, but she let her pent up breath out on a slow sigh. "I'm sure Amy will figure everything out."

"Does she know you want Rick at the table?"

"I'll let her know. We just started dating, Don. We have to find a way to make everything fit too." She glanced at Rick and smiled. "But it'll all work out." She squeezed his hand before she let go of it, and then got to her feet. "Now if there's nothing else, Rick and I have some business to take care of."

"Business? Is that what you call it now?"

"When his construction company is going to be renovating my apartment? Yes."

There was that frown again. "What apartment?"

"Over the shop. That's where I'm going to live. Oh yeah, all that stuff of yours you inconveniently left here is still in the garage. You're going to need to come and get whatever you want or I'll get rid of it."

He growled and strode toward the front door.

"Just call me ahead of time and I'll make sure you can get into the garage." That sounded a little nastier than she'd intended. Eve softened her tone. "I appreciate you wanting to get things settled between us so there's no awkwardness at Amy's wedding."

Don nodded, put his hand on the door knob, and then turned to face Rick. "Best? I'd like to apologize for last night." Don grimaced as he looked at Eve. "I suppose he told you what happened."

She crossed her arms. “That you challenged Rick to a knock-down, drag-out fight at the bar last night? Rick never mentioned it, but plenty of people came into the shop today to tell me about it.”

“I wasn’t really going to fight with him. I had too much to drink.”

“I don’t want to hear about it.” She rubbed the ache between her brows. “Just go home, Don.”

He looked like he was going to say something else, then Don turned and walked out the door. For good, she hoped.

Eve let out a sigh. “Will there ever be a time when we can talk civilly? Will I ever lose this anger?” She didn’t like it, but Don seemed to bring out the worst in her.

Rick put his arm around her. “I don’t know, but it’s early yet. Last year at this time you were still married. It’s going to take a while, I’m sure, to feel comfortable in your new life.” He turned her back into the living room where he’d spread out paperwork and samples over the coffee table.

Her excitement wiped her ex-husband almost completely from her mind.

“You have a lot of choices to make,” Rick told her. “You don’t have to decide everything tonight, but the sooner you do, the sooner we can get everything ordered.”

For the next hour or so they talked pros and cons of different types of flooring and windows and showers. Debated closet options and paint colors to brighten the foyer and landing.

Eve couldn’t help but get turned on by the press of Rick’s hard thigh against hers as they sat side by side on the sofa. The brush of his fingers when they reached for something at the same time sent shivers along her skin. The rumble of his laugh and his masculine scent called to something primal and deep within her. By the time all the decisions were made Eve was filled with a combination of excitement and arousal and plain old happiness.

Apparently Rick brought out the best in her.

After signing the contract, she rose. "I think this calls for wine. Would you like some?" At his nod, she took down two wine glasses from the shelf above the wet bar and slid a bottle of Riesling from the wine fridge underneath.

She turned her head as she asked, "White all right?" and found him right behind her. "Oh! Hi."

"White's fine." He placed his hands on her shoulders and nuzzled her hair. "You smell so good." His warm breath tickled her ear. "You've been driving me crazy tonight. Do you know how difficult it was for me to sit beside you and not touch you?"

She turned into his arms. The wine could wait. "Oh no. You were driving *me* crazy."

"Not as much as you were making me."

She chuckled lightly. "I bet you argued with your brothers all the time. *No, I didn't. Yes, you did.*"

"It's possible." But he didn't laugh. His eyes darkened before his gaze dropped to her lips. "All I could think about was kissing you again. And doing it better than the last time."

Her tongue darted out to wet her lips. She couldn't help it. "I don't know. That was pretty great for a middle-of-an-alley first kiss." She wrapped her arms around his neck. Her heart thudded. "You really think we could do better than that? Now? Here?"

He brushed his lips along her jaw. "I'm certain of it."

Shivers danced along her skin. "I think you're right."

Rick pushed her up against the bar, placing his legs on either side of her. "No argument then?"

"Not from me."

His mouth was on hers before the last word was out of her mouth. Hot and hungry, this kiss was like no other she'd ever had. His teeth took little nips at her mouth, not hard enough to hurt, just little stings that made her catch her breath. Her fingers dug into his shoulders and his tongue laved her lips then, soothing the sting.

Thoughts of Don and renovations were pushed out of her head by a greedy mouth and wandering hands. The room faded away until there was only the two of them wrapped up in a cocoon of sensations.

One of his hands slid up her ribs and cupped her breast. She arched her back instinctively, pressing into his palm. And with the movement, knocked over one of the empty wine glasses with a loud clink.

He backed away. Cleared his throat. "Guess I could use that wine now."

Eve was dizzy with passion. She still gripped his shoulders. "Give me a minute. Your kisses pack quite a punch."

"Yeah?" He grinned, then gave her a quick peck before backing away. "Let me." He opened the wine and poured.

She nearly downed the whole glass in one gulp. What was going on here? Why did what was supposed to be for show suddenly feel surprisingly real? Did she want it to be real?

Eve sat on the sofa beside Rick and sipped her wine as she searched for something to say. After months of being on her own, sitting beside a man in this room seemed strange, even though she'd lived here with Don for twenty-five years. Did she want to get used to being with another guy just when she was enjoying being on her own?

"Rick..." She had to get the ground rules set, even though she knew this was no game.

The phone he'd set on the coffee table buzzed. Rick glanced down to check the text. He groaned and looked back to Eve.

"Well, the word has apparently traveled far and wide. My parents have already heard that you and I are a couple. Max says Mom wants me to bring you over for Sunday dinner."

No. No. This was pretend. This wasn't meet-the-parents dating. She'd known Martha and Ted Best her whole life, of course, but this would be different. Sunday dinner with the family? As Rick's girlfriend?

"I can't," she blurted. "I have plans. Please thank your mother for the invitation but I can't come. Plans."

"Okay." The gaze he pinned her with told her that he knew it was an excuse. He nodded and set his half-empty wine glass on the table. He shoved his phone into his pocket. "It's going to be a long two months if things get this awkward between us every time dating is mentioned."

"I know. You're right." After the incredible kisses they'd just shared, the tension in his voice made her chest clench. "Look, Rick, I'm sorry."

He shoved all the papers into the case and slammed it shut. "Nothing to be sorry about. You're too busy to have dinner with my parents."

"That's not it." She grabbed his hands. The last thing she wanted was to upset him. "I don't want to lie to your parents."

"We don't have to lie." He tightened his fingers on hers. "You and I like each other. We're going to see what happens between us. We're keeping it casual.

That's all we have to say. I'll make sure my mom understands before you come over. No pressure."

"I'm not going to come over, Rick." He looked so disappointed, she lifted her hand and cupped his jaw. "At least not this weekend. It's too soon. Even if this dating thing was real, it would be too soon. Don't you see?"

"Okay, I'll agree with that." He shook his head. "She's seventy-seven. You'd think she'd keep her nose out of our lives."

"She wants her children to be happy." Eve could understand that. If her mom was alive, she'd want the same thing. Eve did want that for her kids.

"And right now none of us are in a relationship. It breaks her heart."

"She loves you." She smiled and he smiled back. At least the tension in his face had disappeared.

"I should go." Rick rose to his feet. "I'll place the orders tomorrow."

"Great. Thanks."

"Just so you know, I haven't changed my mind about us. I want to take you out again. On a real date. I think we could be good together. Very good." He took her hand. "Just promise me one thing."

She couldn't deny the thrill that buzzed up her spine at his words. She wanted to date him. She didn't want to date him. Her brain was doing that wishy-washy thing again. "Promise you what?"

"Don't call me your boyfriend."

She did her best not to frown as she walked with him to the door. "Okay, I won't, but if we were really dating, what would you want me to call you?"

He dropped a kiss on her lips and was out the door. Before he closed it behind him, he said, "Rick."

Chapter Six

It had been a slow Monday at the shop, giving Eve a lot of time for dusting shelves and thinking about Rick. She wondered how Sunday dinner went with his parents and if he'd told his family the truth about their relationship. Or did he let them believe the stories going around town?

Of course, she'd come right out and told Donald that Rick was her boyfriend. She'd surprised herself, but Don had just made her so angry. And Rick was her wedding date, so it only made sense to play it that way. Besides, she'd liked holding Rick's hand, which made her feel almost like he really was her boyfriend.

But then Rick didn't want to be her boyfriend, isn't that what he said? Or did he say he didn't want her *calling* him her boyfriend? Wasn't that the same thing?

She should be happy. She *was* happy. She didn't want a boyfriend anyway.

Tess and Maggie had both called her over the weekend, but she hadn't answered either one of their calls. She didn't know what to tell them.

Then her friends had started texting her with silly things like...

Eve and Rick sitting in a tree, k-i-s-s-i-n-g...

And straight to the point texts like...

You and Rick Best? That was fast!

She sent them each a text promising to talk to them at dinner on Wednesday. And hoped she'd know what to say by then.

Eve had just locked up the shop when her phone rang. She smiled. She hadn't talked to Seth in a couple of weeks. "Hey, sweetie."

"When were you going to tell me you're selling our house?"

The tight anger in her son's voice sent motherly guilt roiling in her stomach, "Oh, Seth, I was going to call you. I've just been so busy."

"Too busy to let me know you're selling all my memories? I can't believe you'd do that."

She sank into a small slipper chair tucked in the corner by the china tea sets. "It's too much house for me, honey. And you know you're going to have your memories with you forever. Nothing can take them away from you."

"You can't sell the house, Mom. That's our home."

She wasn't going to let him keep playing on her guilt, even though she could understand his feelings. "You moved out of the house, remember? Moved all the way to San Diego."

"But I thought it would always be there to come home to." The anger had left his voice and melancholy had taken over.

"And I thought I'd live there forever," she told him gently, "but things happen." *Like your father leaving me for another woman.* "Things change. Sometimes our lives fall apart and when they get put back together, they don't look the same anymore. But we still live them the best we can. And maybe they'll be even better than they were before if we give them a chance."

"I'm sorry, Mom. I didn't think." Seth had always been the calm one. The calm after the storm that was Hurricane Amy. Eve was glad the composed Seth was back. "How are you doing?" he went on. "I never thought about you being all alone in that big house. I can see how you wouldn't want to keep doing that."

"Thanks for understanding." Her little boy sounded so grown up. Of course, he was. He was twenty-four and working for a software company in California. But to her, he'd always be her little boy. "Tess has already shown the house several times. She promises even if we had an offer today, we wouldn't have to worry about moving out until after the wedding. You have a lot of stuff still here. When you come back for the wedding, you'll need to spend some time going through it all. Decide what you want to keep and what can go."

"Amy said you're going to move into the apartment over your shop. I remember playing up there when I was little. Do you really want to live there? It's pretty small."

"It's the perfect size for me. And I'm having some updates done. Best Brothers is doing the work. I'm so excited about it."

"I'm glad you're happy, Mom. Really." He cleared his throat. "Okay, now that that's out of the way, when were you going to tell me about you and Rick Best?"

So word had spread all the way across the country. "You and your sister had quite a talk, didn't you?"

"Well, she talked mostly about the wedding."

Eve chuckled. "It's consumed her life. Thank goodness there are only a few more weeks to go. I am looking forward to seeing you soon. I miss you."

"Miss you too, but I still want to hear about you and Mr. Best."

She didn't want to lie to her son, so she kept to the truth. "We went out to dinner. Once. At the BB&G.

Nothing fancy."

"But I hear he's your date to the wedding."

"Well, yes, he is. I like him." She shrugged, even though Seth couldn't see her. With a quick change of subject, she asked, "How's the job going?"

They chatted a few minutes more about his new job, new apartment, new life far away, and after they said their good-byes, Eve was abruptly swept up by empty-nester tears. She grabbed her purse and dashed up the stairs. Rick's crew had left a little while ago, so she wouldn't be in their way. She hoped by looking at the progress they'd made, she could stop grieving for her old life, stop wishing her kids were little again, and look forward to the future she was making for herself.

As soon as she stepped into the kitchen, she knew she wasn't alone. She heard footsteps in the bedroom. She swiped away the tears from her face as best she could. "Hello?"

Rick stepped through the doorway. "Hi."

"I thought everyone had gone." She sniffed and turned away from him, hoping he wouldn't have noticed she'd been crying. "Wow, pantry shelves already?"

All the demolition had been completed to make space for the shower. It looked like today the new pantry had been built.

"Are you okay?" He came up behind her, placed his hands on her shoulders and turned her around. "You're crying?"

She sniffed. "Not anymore."

"What's the matter?"

"Just talked to Seth and it hit me how much I miss him."

Rick gathered her into his arms. "I think I'd have a really hard time if Heather moved away. Of course you miss him."

She nodded into his shoulder. When she lifted her

head she saw his shirt was wet. She brushed her hand over the damp spot, as if she could wipe it away. "Sorry, I didn't expect the tears today. He's been in San Diego six months."

Rick lifted her chin with one finger and dropped a kiss to her lips. She wrapped her arms around his neck and kissed him back because she couldn't resist.

When she began to feel overwhelmed, by his taste and by the arousal running through her veins, she pulled back just enough to look into his eyes. "Did you intend to distract me with that kiss?"

He grinned and the crinkles around his eyes made her melt a little more. "Maybe. Did it work?"

"Yeah." She smiled against his lips and dove in again. A little warning bell rang in the back of her head but she didn't want to listen to it now. He tasted too delicious. And his hard body felt so good against hers.

His hands swept up and down her back as he nibbled on her lips. He pressed close enough that she could feel the hardness of his erection against her hip. Her body reacted, softening. Tingling. It had been a long time since she'd had sex. She wasn't sure she wanted to go to bed with Rick quite yet. But she realized she was open to the possibility in the near future.

And the thought scared her. She reluctantly pulled away. She wasn't ready for that much intimacy yet.

"Eve, would you like to—" Rick broke off as the phone in his pocket let out a loud wail. He dropped a kiss to the top of her head and let her go. He dug the phone out and looked at the screen, then sent her an apologetic glance. "Sorry. Rescue call. I have to go."

She nodded, disappointed, yet a little relieved. "Be careful."

"I'll talk to you soon."

***

An hour later, Rick pulled his truck into the garage.

Old Edgar Gates had been a little shaky and confused, but that was probably because he'd been out weeding all day in the heat. Once he got some fluids pumped into him in the ER, he should be fine. Twenty-five years from now, Rick figured he'd be the one resisting hiring help to do the things he'd done his entire life.

Growing old sucked.

He'd thought about stopping at the BB&G for dinner, but he didn't feel like eating alone. Well, at least he didn't want to *eat out* by himself. Nowadays he almost always ate alone. Rick wandered into the kitchen and opened the fridge. Nothing looked appetizing. He could have been chowing down on a BB&G burger right now. He'd often gone out to eat by himself after Cathy had been killed, so when had that changed?

He knew when. Since he'd had dinner with Eve. Since he'd held her hand. Kissed her. Pressed her body against his.

Held her while she cried.

He'd been going to ask Eve to join him for dinner when the call came through. The kitchen lights were on in the house next door, so he was sure she would have already eaten something by now. Another time then.

Rick pulled some leftover chicken out of the fridge and chewed on it while he thought again about Eve in his arms. Her soft body had pressed against him like a promise. Her mouth had opened to him like an offering. The little moan she made in the back of her throat made him want to lift her into his arms and carry her to the bed.

Except there was no bed in her apartment. No furniture at all. He didn't want the first time he made love to Eve to be on a scuffed hardwood floor.

The back door opened. "Hello?" It was Heather.

"In the kitchen!"

His daughter swept into the room and into his

arms. After a quick hug she stepped away and looked at the solitary piece of cold chicken lying on the plate on the counter. "Great dinner, Dad. Hope you don't always eat like this."

Rick shrugged. "Didn't have anyone to cook for. Have you eaten?"

She sent him a mischievous glance. "Just a little leftover chicken too."

He laughed. "Spaghetti?" It had been their go-to meal when Cathy'd gone to her once-a- month garden club meetings. Heather nodded and then pitched in to help.

They chatted about her husband Ryan and how scared she was each time he put on his police uniform and left her to keep the community safe. How glad she was that they lived in a small town like Best Bay, because he had less of a chance of being hurt in the line of duty. Rick didn't say much, just listened as she poured out her fears and her love for her husband.

And as they sat down to eat, she said, "I think we want to start a family."

His little girl. But Rick wasn't surprised. "How exciting."

"But, I don't know. Ryan and I have been talking about it for a while, but it never seems like the right time, you know? There was buying the house. And then we needed a new car. Then I finally got the full-time position at the school and Ryan's job is so dangerous, and one thing always leads to another and I don't know if it's the right time."

"Sweetie, don't wait for the right time. If you do, it'll never happen."

"I know but—"

"Life is a series of things happening, one right after another. If you want to start a family, go for it. There will never be a perfect time."

Heather chuckled. "Yeah, I guess you're right. It's kinda scary though. Having a child."

"It's terrifying." Rick stroked her bright red hair. "And it's more wonderful than you can imagine. You'll be a great mom. I just wish your mom could be here to give you her motherly advice."

"I know, but you give great advice too." She leaned over and kissed his cheek. "I'm glad I came over tonight."

"So am I."

"Hey, I guess you took *my* advice about something, Dad."

"What advice?"

"Asking Mrs. C. out on a date. I heard you two went out to dinner."

He sighed. "It wasn't really a date. More like a business dinner."

"I heard handholding was involved." She crinkled her nose up the way she liked to do when she thought of something funny. "Doesn't sound like business, unless it was monkey business."

Rick shook his head and chuckled. If he was more certain of how Eve felt, he'd be more comfortable talking to his daughter. Instead, he felt on edge, waiting for Eve to tell him to take a hike. "I'm going to be her date for Amy's wedding, so that should make you happy."

"It does!" She linked her fingers together as if she were praying. "Amy and I have always wanted to be sisters since we were little girls. Now maybe—"

"Whoa. Hold on. Let's not go there yet." It was way too early, but the idea of marrying Eve, of them living together, sharing the rest of their lives, didn't freak him out like he thought it would have.

"Okay, but Ryan and I have been talking about having a cook-out. He wants to try out his new grill.

Why don't you and Mrs. C. come over Saturday afternoon? We'll invite Amy and Blake. Just for fun. You can bring a salad."

"A salad? Seriously?"

There was that crinkly nose again. "Mrs. C. makes the best salads."

Apparently even his daughter was going to treat them like a couple. "I'll ask her." He wanted to ask Eve out again anyway.

"Call her now."

"Heather..." How many fathers called for a date while their daughters were in the same room?

She crossed her arms and batted her eyelashes. "Dad..." He'd never been able to resist when she fluttered those lashes.

Rick sighed but pulled out his phone and called Eve. When she answered, just the sound of her voice sent unexpected pleasure flowing over him. "Hi."

"How was the rescue call?" she asked.

"Edgar Gates was trying to do too much and collapsed. I think he'll be okay."

"I hope so."

"Listen, Eve, Heather is here and she's planning a cook-out on Saturday and she wants me to invite you."

"That was a horrible invitation. Let me talk to her." Heather grabbed the phone. "Hey, Mrs. C. It's nothing fancy, burgers on the grill and beer in the cooler." She paused while she listened to whatever Eve was saying. "Come on, Mrs. C. It's just for fun. I'm going to invite Amy and Blake too if they're not busy. You can bring that kick-ass salad with the mandarin oranges and almonds, remember that one?" Heather's eyes brightened and Rick knew Eve had agreed. "Great. You and Dad can come any time after two o'clock. Perfect. Thanks! See you then." Heather sent Rick a triumphant look as she disconnected and then handed him back his phone. “All set.”

“You learned that railroading technique from your mother, didn’t you?”

She grinned. “Maybe.”

Heather helped him with the clean-up and then was out the door, leaving him alone, but with a smile on his face.

***

Wednesday came before she knew it. As she walked to O’Neill’s from her shop, Eve still wasn’t sure how much she was going to admit to Maggie and Tess about her relationship with Rick. But when the time came, and she was sitting across the table from them, Eve knew she had to be truthful with her friends. They’d understand. If anyone could be trusted to give her advice, it was these women.

“It just happened,” she explained. “It was past dinnertime by the time we finished talking about the work I wanted done on the apartment, so we decided to stop at the BB&G. Donald came in and started acting all caveman, announcing to the entire place that he didn’t like the fact that we were a couple. So we decided to play along. Played it up if you really want to know. It just happened,” she repeated.

“So you’re pretending?” Maggie pouted. “I’m disappointed. I thought you were going to be happy. I thought you two would make a great couple.”

Tess narrowed her eyes. “*Are* you pretending? Or is there more you’re not telling us?”

“Um...” Eve took another sip of wine.

“The truth now.”

This was the part that was hard to know what to say. Hard to know what the truth was. “Well, Rick wants to date for real.”

Maggie squealed like she had back in high school. What was it about talking about guys that turned grown women into teenagers again?

"I like him. A lot. But it's not the right time." When both her friends just sat there with raised brows, waiting for her to go on, Eve said, "I don't want to go out with anyone right now. I'm just getting used to being on my own. I like being on my own. A guy would just mess things up."

"Tess goes out with guys all the time and she's still on her own."

"True." Eve turned to Tess. "Why is that? You've never dated the same guy more than once or twice in all the time I've known you." Tess hadn't grown up in Best Bay like Maggie and Eve had, but she'd moved there almost twenty years ago.

"Guess I haven't found the right person yet."

"Maybe she does bat for the other team. Oh, sweetie, do you like women but didn't know how to tell us? Because you know we'd love you no matter what." Maggie's face turned bright pink. "Well, not *love* you in that way because I definitely crush on guys, but you know what I mean."

"If I was a lesbian, you'd know." Tess downed the rest of her wine and gestured for another one. "And I wouldn't hide it by dating men. Or be afraid to let everyone know."

"You're the bravest person I know," Maggie told her. "You're not afraid of anything."

"You face a room full of five-year-olds every day," Tess countered. "You're the brave one."

Eve sat back and listened to her friends banter, glad the conversation had moved on from her and Rick. She honestly didn't know what to say. Could it work with Rick? Did she want it to? Would a few dates to test the waters hurt anything? Or would it ruin their friendship if things didn't work out?

And would she find herself back in her old life,

catering to a man and losing that independence she was finally embracing?

Tess's phone vibrated. "Sorry. Let me check this." She glanced at the screen and she smiled. "We have an offer."

"Already?"

"I told you it would go fast." She tossed her phone into her purse. "Tomorrow is soon enough to think about it, but..." Tess waved the waiter over. Shawn, Eve's former paperboy, came over to the table.

"Some dessert, ladies?"

"A bottle of champagne."

"Oh, Tess, isn't it a little soon for that?"

"No. This is a couple with two young children and they're offering your asking price. Are you going to say no to that?"

"Of course not."

"Then let's celebrate."

"You sold your house?" Shawn asked.

Eve nodded. Tears prickled her eyes even though she was happy the house had sold quickly. Really happy. She'd been way too teary lately.

Maggie noticed and grasped her hand. "Change is hard. Even change we're happy about."

"Gee, Mrs. Corcoran. It won't be the same without you on the street."

Eve studied Shawn. "And how soon before you move away from Best Bay?"

"Um. I'm moving to Buffalo next month to finish my degree at UB."

"See. You won't be living on our street anymore, either."

"Guess not. Wow. It's starting to feel real." He cleared his throat. "I'll get you that bottle of champagne, ladies."

"You okay, Eve?" Maggie asked.

"Yeah." She agreed with Shawn. "It's just starting to feel real."

Chapter Seven

Eve was surprised when Rick came into her shop early the next morning. He had a big grin on his face and she couldn't help but return his smile. His black T-shirt clung to his sculpted torso and his faded jeans highlighted his long, lean legs. He sure didn't look like a guy who spent most of his time behind a desk.

She was ringing out Melissa O'Neill, owner of the restaurant where Eve and her friends met every Wednesday. Mel was picking up a gift for her parents' upcoming fiftieth wedding anniversary. She ruffled her fingers through her short pixie cut as she grumbled about the fact that she was losing a couple of her servers next month when they left to attend colleges out of town. Eve knew Shawn was one of them.

"And that's so soon after Rob and Jami left me for Hollywood, of all places. I'm going to have to advertise for help again. And train more help again. Kids don't want to stay around small towns any more, do they?"

"A lot of kids left when we were their age too," Eve replied. "Looking for more excitement than they can get here, I guess." She cut her gaze to Rick. Eve didn't have to mention his brother, Noah, by name. Noah had broken his engagement to Mel twenty years ago and left

Best Bay behind. He'd rarely been back since.

"You're right, of course. If you hear of anyone looking for restaurant work, send them my way." Mel picked up her package. "Thanks. See you later." She turned to leave and saw Rick standing there. She looked back to Eve. "So the talk about you two is true?"

"I guess it depends on what the talk is," Eve said, but she couldn't stop a silly grin from lifting her lips. She wanted to slap her hand across her mouth to hide it, but it was too late.

"Oh yeah," Mel said, her eyes wide. "It's true." She smiled. "Good luck to you." She took a couple of steps, then stopped again. "What do you hear from Noah?" she asked Rick.

"Not much, Mel. He never was much for talking. You know that."

"Still alive?"

Rick raised a brow. "Last I knew."

"Good. I guess. I haven't seen your folks in a while. Tell them I say hi."

"I will."

She nodded. "Well, bye."

Eve watched Mel stride from the shop. "You ever hear what happened? Between her and Noah?"

"Nope. Noah was always a dreamer. Not Mel. She's the practical type. I figure they realized they were too different. Last Mom said, he's working in a restaurant down south somewhere. I don't think she even knows where. He might have moved on by now. No clue if that was his dream or not."

"I hope so." Eve remembered the quiet, good-looking Best brother. The youngest until John came along. She wondered if there was more to the story since Noah never came around, never caught up with old friends. Or family. But it wasn't any of Eve's business. Maybe someday Rick would tell her about it.

Or maybe there was nothing to tell.

Eve stepped around the counter and found herself in Rick's arms. "Hi. This was a nice surprise."

"Thought you'd like to know your window is here."

She gasped. "Already?"

"Come up after you close tonight. It should be installed by then."

She wanted to jump up and down with delight, but she restrained herself. "I can't wait to see it. Will you be there?"

He brushed his lips over hers. "I can be."

"Good." *Good?* Yeah, it was. She'd be lying if she said she wasn't looking forward to seeing Rick every bit as much as she wanted to see her new window. Hadn't she told herself a few dates wouldn't hurt anything? Hadn't she stepped right into his arms?

"How about dinner afterward?" he asked.

"Well..."

He toyed with the tips of her hair. "We'll be hungry. Everyone in town is already sure we're dating, so it won't be a surprise for anyone to see us together."

"I know." Eve brushed some nonexistent fuzz off his shirt. Damn, she liked the way she felt in his arms. "You're right. Sure. I'd love to have dinner with you tonight."

"Good," he said. Guess he was looking forward to seeing her too.

The bell rang over the door and she reluctantly stepped away from him. Mel's parents, Phyllis and Rory O'Neill, strolled through arm in arm. They bought each other an anniversary gift from her shop every year.

Eve turned to Rick. "I'll see you around five then."

He shot her a grin, and then she watched him stop to talk with the O'Neills before he left the shop. Eve realized she couldn't pull her attention away from the guy she was beginning to like more than she should.

What was she going to do about it?

***

Cathy had never described Rick as being romantic, but then he'd really never had to seduce her, not even at the beginning. As he carried his supplies up the stairs to Eve's apartment, he smiled, remembering Cathy coming up to him on the first day of community college and asking him to help her find the Intro to Biology class. He'd been just as lost as she was, but he'd been looking for the same room, so they searched through the halls together and were only a little late to the first class.

She'd asked him to join her for lunch afterward. And they'd pretty much been together for the next thirty years.

Things with Eve were different. He had to make more of an effort this time and if his brothers wanted to razz him about it, that was okay. He liked working for what he desired. He liked thinking about seducing her.

Rick made sure his guys had finished both the installation and clean up with plenty of time to spare. Then he laid the scene. He was putting on the final touches when he heard her footsteps on the stairs.

He quickly lit the candles on the counter, and since he'd already hooked up his phone to the portable mini-speakers Heather had given him last year for Christmas, he just had to push the play arrow to start the music he'd downloaded.

Eve opened the door. "Rick?" Then she gasped and dashed across the room. "What did you do? Candles? Music?"

"I thought instead of going out to eat, we could have a picnic in front of your new window."

"The window! It's perfect." Her hands went to her cheeks. "Look at it. It's so big. I can see everything. The beautiful garden." She turned to face him. "Thank you.

It's so much better than I ever expected. I can't wait to get a table and chairs. But for now..." She crouched down and swept her hand over the red plaid blanket he'd spread on the floor in front of the window. She looked up at him. "Is there anything I can do to help?"

"Would you want to grab a couple of beers from the fridge while I get the food?" Rick grabbed the insulated bag he'd picked up from the BB&G. "Nothing fancy. Pulled pork sandwiches and fries."

"Sounds great. I'm starved." Eve grabbed the bottles of beer he'd put in the fridge earlier and carried them over to the spot by the window.

Rick froze as he watched her kick off her heels, lower gracefully to the blanket and then tuck her legs under her full skirt. After a moment, he shook himself and got back on task. He placed the food on paper plates and grabbed the napkins Jimmy had put in the bag. Then he carried them over to the blanket and knelt across from her.

It was still light outside, so he didn't really need the candles, but he could swear the flicker of the candlelight sparkled in her eyes. Her smile was brilliant and he had a feeling his first attempt at being romantic was a huge success. Conversation halted as they dug into their sandwiches. They listened to 70s and 80s love songs while they ate. She hummed along to Billy Joel and Carly Simon, Lionel Richie and Heart.

"I love this music," Eve told him. "Guess you know you've gotten old when you enjoy the old songs more than the new ones."

He locked her gaze with his. "You're not old, Eve."

"Some days I feel like it."

He let his eyes travel over her. The slight lines on her face and experience in her eyes simply made her more attractive to him.

Eve cleared her throat, pulled her gaze away and

looked out the window. "I can't believe you went to all this trouble." She took another bite of sandwich.

"It wasn't that much trouble. Believe it or not, I didn't do the cooking. I hit Jimmy up for most of this stuff."

"Really?" Eve chuckled. "It took a lot of thought and I appreciate it." She reached out and placed her hand over his. "Thank you. For the window and the picnic."

He curled his fingers over hers. "I was glad to do it. And this way I get to have you all to myself. No neighbors trying to eavesdrop. No one craning their neck to get a look at us. Pretty soon we'll be old news, but for now, I enjoy the chance to be alone with you."

He leaned over and kissed her. The tangy BBQ sauce gave a unique flavor to the kiss. Eve hummed and kissed him back, her hand still grasping his. Her tongue dueled with his. Their moans harmonized even as they were lost in the kiss.

Rick was breathing heavily when he finally pulled away. Eve was doing the same. He cleared his throat. "Guess we should finish eating."

Eve nodded. "It is delicious." She picked up the sandwich, but her hands seemed to tremble slightly as she took another bite. "How was Sunday dinner?"

It took a few seconds for Rick to process the change of subject. "Fine. Mom understood that you didn't feel comfortable coming over and she apologized for pushing."

"You were supposed to tell her I was busy."

"I did, but apparently busy is a universal excuse."

"What if I was actually busy?"

"Guess you'd need to come up with another excuse. Because I don't think she'll believe that. Or you could just come for dinner next time. Really, Mom's a great cook and nothing makes her happier than feeding as many people as possible."

"You do this every Sunday?"

"Pretty much. Unless we're *busy*."

Eve rolled her eyes and laughed. At least she seemed more relaxed with him than she had been earlier. Rick hoped that meant she thought dating was a good idea. A great idea.

Because he sure did.

***

She was weakening. Eve could tell Rick was beginning to wear down her resistance. How could she hang onto her independence if he kept doing things like this? Candlelight flickering around the room. Oldies playing through tiny speakers. Casual meal and easy conversation.

Who knew he was a romantic?

When they'd finished eating, Rick reached for the plates, but she pushed his hands away. "I'll do that." She gathered up the paper plates and napkins, got to her feet and threw them in the trash. Easy clean-up.

Rick rose too. "Want another beer?"

Stay strong. "I should probably head home."

"Already?" He took her hand. "Let's take advantage of the lack of furniture." He pulled her into his arms and began to move to Air Supply's "The One That You Love". They fit together as if they belonged and she didn't want to think too hard about that. "Perfect dance floor, don't you think?" he added.

Eve nodded and rested her head on his shoulder. Rick was a few years older than her, so they'd never run in the same circles in school. They'd never had the chance to dance like this in the school gym. She closed her eyes and savored the movement of their bodies, pressed close to one another, brushing against each other as they moved.

The hardwood floor was smooth under her bare feet. She slipped her hands under his T-shirt where his skin was smooth under her fingers. Her body was slowly warming and it wasn't all from body heat. She couldn't help but nuzzle his neck, running her lips along his salty skin. Her breasts pillowed against his hard chest and they tingled with the need for even more stimulation.

They were barely moving now. Rick's erection pressed into her and she rocked her pelvis, pressing back. He drove his fingers into her hair and angled her head for a deep kiss. REO Speedwagon's "Can't Fight This Feeling" began to play and Eve found herself embracing the sentiment.

The little voice in the back of her mind reminded her that there was no way things could work between them. Not long term. Rick might not be as controlling as her father or Donald. But he was still a take-charge kind of guy. She'd had enough of those kind of guys.

But right now it was easy to ignore that whisper. To hum along with the music and drown out the voice of reason. This dance wasn't about reason. It was about emotion. Sensation. Arousal. Pleasure.

She didn't want to fight her feelings right now.

"Rick..." She cupped his face and kissed him again.

Rick cupped her bottom, began to scooch up the fabric of her skirt with his fingers. "I want you so much," he groaned, but then he dropped his hands before his fingers touched bare skin. She whimpered. "I don't want to rush you, Eve. I'm willing to wait until you're ready."

"I don't want to wait." The words came out in a rush. If she waited, that voice in the back of her head might get louder and she didn't want that. At least not tonight. Tomorrow would be soon enough to worry about choices and independence. She stepped back into his arms. "I want you too."

Rick crushed his lips to hers and she fell into him.

The blanket seemed too far away at the moment. He could take her against the wall and she'd be happy.

And then she heard the outside door open downstairs and Tess called out her name. Eve groaned and broke away from Rick, breathing heavily. "I need to start locking that door."

"Eve? Are you here?" Footsteps started up the stairs.

Eve sighed. "Up here."

Tess opened the door to the kitchen and glanced from Eve to Rick and back again. Eve wondered what she looked like. Hair wild from Rick's fingers? Lips swollen from his kisses? Shirt askew from his hands exploring beneath?

"I saw the lights on up here. You didn't answer your phone."

"It's in my purse down in my office." She'd had other things on her mind at closing time.

"Oh, hello, Rick." Tess didn't hide the hint of amusement on her face. "Sorry if I interrupted. Eve, I thought you wanted to look over the contract."

"Contract?" Rick asked.

"Oh yeah." She turned to him. "I sold the house."

He put his hand on her arm as if he felt the need to stay connected. "Congratulations. But it won't be the same without you next door."

Nothing was going to be the same ever again. "I keep telling myself that change is good."

Rick's lips quirked. "It can be. Sometimes we have to work at it."

"And sometimes it just falls into place." She hoped.

"Hey guys, remember me?" Tess called out. "Your neighborly realtor? Contract?"

Eve glanced at Rick before she turned to Tess. "Can't it wait until the morning?" She still wanted Rick. Sex with Rick.

Tess raised a brow. "You want to get together early, before you open the shop tomorrow?"

Eve wasn't about to send Rick home now. If she was lucky it would be a late night, but she had a feeling it would be worth it.

"I'll bring coffee and muffins," Eve promised.

"Okay, my office at seven thirty?"

"See you then."

"Good night, guys." Tess smiled. "Don't do anything I wouldn't do."

"Fat chance," Eve murmured as Tess closed the door behind her.

Rick ran his hands through his hair. He looked as frustrated as she felt. "Need a new lock for that door?"

"No. I lock it when I leave. I guess I don't think about it when I'm here."

He reached into his pocket and pulled out the spare key she'd given him the other day. It was obviously not a shiny new key. "Don't you change it every time your tenants leave?"

"I don't have to. I always get the keys back."

"You're too trusting. Keys can be lost. Duplicated."

"Oh, you're right." Why hadn't she thought of that? Maybe she *was* too trusting. "I'll get a new lock this weekend."

He placed a hand on her shoulder. "I'll do it for you."

She knew Rick didn't mean it in the superior I'll-take-care-of-everything way that Don always used, but still it was an I-like-to-take-charge tone of voice. Why did no one think she was capable of taking care of things herself? She shrugged his hand off her shoulder. "No, that's okay."

"Eve, my guys can get the new lock set and take care of it when they come to work in the morning."

"I can get my own damn lock."

Rick raised his hands in surrender. "Okay. I was just trying to help."

"I don't need your help. I can take care of it myself." And as Eve listened to herself she knew she was over-reacting. She closed her eyes for a moment, then reached for him but he turned away and grabbed the blanket off the floor.

When he faced her again, she thought his stubborn expression might have masked a bit of hurt. "You didn't sell your house by yourself, did you?" Rick didn't look at her as he spoke, but focused on folding the blanket. "You didn't show the house to potential buyers. You didn't negotiate the price. You didn't write up the contract. Did you?"

"No, but—"

He set the folded blanket on the counter and finally looked at her. His jaw was tight. "You could have. But you didn't. You let Tess do it. Because that's her job. And even though you could have done the work yourself, you let someone who was experienced help you."

She sighed. "Okay, you've made your point."

"I don't want to have to worry about everything I say to you. I don't want you to snap at me and take my words the wrong way if I offer to help you with something."

"I'm sorry." She had hurt him and she wished she could take back her words. But maybe it was better this way. "I don't know how to do this. Maybe I shouldn't even try."

"This? What is *this*? You and me? Or sex? Did you pick a fight with me just so we wouldn't have sex?"

"No! God, I'm so horny I can barely stand up. That is, until I over-reacted. I'm sorry, Rick. You didn't deserve that. If you could take care of changing the lock I'd appreciate it."

He studied her for a moment. “You’re sure you’re ready for sex?”

She huffed. “I was ready to have sex against the wall until Tess interrupted us.”

“The first time with you is not going to be up against the wall.” He chuckled a bit sadly. “In fact, I’m afraid my sex-against-the-wall days may be over.”

“How are your sex-in-a-bed days?”

He smiled as his gaze heated. “Why don’t you let me know?”

Chapter Eight

Rick followed Eve as they drove the few miles from the center of the village to the cul-de-sac they'd both called home for many years. It would seem strange for a new family to live next door, but Rick planned to still be seeing Eve often.

Eve pulled into her garage, but instead of entering her house, she walked over to meet him at his. He'd never noticed how sexy her walk was before and he took advantage of the time to stand on the blacktop and watch the way her hips swayed as she approached. His body was reacting again, hardening as he looked forward to going to bed with this beautiful woman.

The argument they had about the lock worried him. He'd never known Eve to be a prickly sort of woman before. He understood that she was worried about being able to take care of herself and make her own choices. He hoped she'd be able to find a balance between holding on to her independence and allowing people – especially him – into her life. Otherwise he was afraid a relationship with Eve wouldn't work out after all. He was a straight talking guy. He wasn't going to watch his words around her for the rest of his life.

At the moment, though, she'd reached his driveway.

He met her at the edge and slipped his arm around her waist. Without a word, he ushered her into the garage and pushed the button to close the door behind them.

The house was dark and quiet when they entered. He hated it that way. He should have left a couple of lights on. Rick flipped the switch for the kitchen lights and then turned to study Eve. She stood just inside the doorway and he couldn't decipher her mood from her expression. He hoped to hell she hadn't changed her mind. He took a couple of eager steps toward her and she tensed. Okay...time to back off.

He wanted nothing more than to scoop her into his arms and carry her to his bedroom like a caveman. He figured his cavemen days were behind him, just like his sex-against-the-wall days. But he hoped like hell he had years and years of sex-in-a-bed-and-other-places still ahead of him.

Rick gestured toward the refrigerator. "Thirsty?"

"Only for you." Then Eve rolled her eyes. "Pretty lame, huh? I haven't dated in a really long time."

"Just be yourself, Eve. We've known each other too long for anything else."

She nodded. "Then I can admit I'm a little nervous?" He must have frowned because she held up her hand as if to stop his forehead from wrinkling. "I'm not saying I don't want to have sex with you because I do. But..." She placed her palm over his heart. "Could we slow things down a little? Maybe start with another kiss?"

"Of course." Instead of diving right into another kiss, Rick lifted his hands and stroked her hair gently away from her face. "You're so pretty. So soft." He cupped her face with both hands and started with a soft kiss. "I'm glad you're here."

"I'm glad too."

He hadn't spent the length of the drive getting

nervous as Eve apparently had. Instead, anticipation had been sending his blood pumping south. He was ready to take her to bed right this minute. But he'd had sex occasionally since his wife died, with women he'd dated short-term. Evidently Eve hadn't had sex with anyone but her husband since college. Of course, she'd be nervous. Rick needed to make sure she was aroused enough that there would be no room for anxiety. The last thing he wanted was to scare her away.

Rick took her hand and led her into the great room off the kitchen. He didn't turn on the lights. There was enough of a glow from the kitchen for them to see where they were going and he thought she might be more comfortable in the shadows.

He'd have to hope that he'd be able to get a better look at her later. Because he was looking forward to that. A lot.

Eve turned into his arms and wrapped her arms around his neck. There was no evidence of nerves as she melted against him. Her soft body went liquid, her curves flowed and molded along his as if they were two parts of a whole finally coming together.

He lowered his mouth to hers once more. She tasted so sweet.

She nodded and swept her palms over his chest. "You make me all shivery."

"That's a good thing?"

"Oh yeah. It's been...." She looked away from him and he caught a glimpse of those nerves. "It's been a long time since I've felt shivery."

"You send my blood pumping." That was an understatement.

Eve ran her hands down his arms. "That's obviously a good thing."

"Definitely." He dropped his hands and stepped back before he grabbed her and probably killed them both by actually attempting sex against the wall. She wanted to take things slow. What could he do to heat her up? Necking on the couch was too high school. He looked across the room and smiled.

He took Eve by the shoulders and turned her to face the bank of windows that looked out over the fenced yard that backed on a stand of evergreen trees that divided them from the houses on the next street. A security light glowed from the far corner of the property. He came up behind her and slipped his arms around her waist. She leaned back against him. Their reflections in the glass shone back at them.

His lips brushed her ear as he whispered, "Look, Eve. Look at us." He caressed her arms with long, slow strokes. "We're taking it slow."

She took a deep, shaky breath, but she didn't tense up or move away. How far could they go? How long would she watch? How long would she let him stoke her fire?

Rick slowly slipped his hands under her silky blouse, skating his fingertips along her warm skin. His palms slid along her flat abdomen. Eve sighed and dropped her head back against his shoulder.

He brushed her ear with his lips. "I'm going to take your top off now."

She caught his gaze reflected in the window as he paused and waited for her response. She nodded slowly and he released a shaky breath. So far, so good.

His fingers tangled with the tips of her silky hair as he grasped the tiny zipper tab at the back of her neck. The fabric parted as he lowered the short zipper. Then he placed a light kiss to her spine before he curled his fingers beneath the hem. She raised her arms and let him strip the lightweight shirt from her body. He tossed it behind them and met her eyes in the reflection again. A lacy white bra hugged the curves of her breasts.

Silently, he reached around her and cupped her with his hands, watched her expression change to arousal as he thumbed her nipples through the lace.

Her breath caught on a ragged gasp and she arched her back slightly, pressing her breasts into his hands and her ass against his crotch. Her hands came around behind her and she grasped his thighs. She whispered his name.

He hardened further behind his fly, the throb quick and insistent, but he didn't want this to be quick. This was their first time together. He wanted it to be special. He wanted to spend time exploring her delectable body and show her how good they could be together.

They were still watching each other's reflections in the window. Eve reached down to unzip her skirt.

He caught her hands, lifted them to his lips and kissed the tips of her fingers. "I'll do it," he murmured and waited for her to protest.

Eve opened her mouth. Then closed it. She dropped her hands to her sides and licked her lips. "Okay."

Rick skimmed his fingers along her ribs as he made his way down to the zipper at the side of her skirt. A part of him wanted to yank that zipper down and take the skirt with it. But another part, masochistic though it may be, wanted to draw this out. To savor the anticipation.

So he slid a finger inside the waistband and drew the tip along her bare abdomen. He felt her stomach tighten, her body tremble. With his other hand, he followed the curve of her bottom, cupping her ass cheek through the fabric.

"Rick?"

"What, sweetheart?" The endearment slipped out so easily, he might have called her that a hundred times before.

She looked at him over her shoulder. "What are you

doing?"

"Keep your eyes on the window," he said and he was happy to see she didn't hesitate to turn her eyes back to their reflections. He smiled. "What am I doing?" he repeated. "I'm taking things slow, just like you asked."

Her hands curled into fists at her sides as he bunched the back of her skirt up to reveal matching white lace panties. Eve began to turn again to look behind her, but he stopped her with his hands on her hips. "Not yet," he said, but he knew she was getting impatient. He'd drawn this out as long as he could. He dropped the skirt and lowered the zipper. The skirt rustled to the floor. Eve stepped out of the crumpled fabric and toed it to the side.

"Oh, Eve." From his vantage point he could see both front and back views of Eve at the same time. Standing there in her lacy white underwear, she was the prettiest thing he'd seen in ages. "What an image you make. What a beautiful woman you are."

Rick pressed up against her back, then reached around her, pinning her against him. He slid one hand down her abdomen and between her thighs, cupping her mound, the panties hot and damp. Oh God, she made him so hard.

She gasped and looked back at him from the window, wide-eyed. "Rick..."

She didn't pull away though. Her ass rubbed against his aching erection with each rock of her hips. He didn't know how much longer he could keep this up.

He scrubbed a hand over his face. "How's that fire going? Are you stoked yet?"

At first she appeared confused, but then she laughed. "Yes." She turned around and crushed her mouth to his in a quick kiss. "The fire is blazing."

"Good, because to be honest, if I had to take things

any slower I might self-combust."

She let out a surprised bark of a laugh. "We don't want that. I want to be the one to make you combust."

Rick chuckled. "I can't wait to feel you come apart in my arms."

Eve moaned. "No one's ever talked to me like this."

"I'm sorry?"

"I didn't think real guys said those sexy, sensual things out loud. I thought it was only in books and movies."

He pulled her into his arms. "I'm flesh and blood, sweetheart."

"Oh, I know." A little frown appeared between her brows. "Why are you fully dressed while I'm in my underwear?"

"I agree, that's definitely wrong. You're still in your underwear." Rick hooked his finger beneath the band of her bra. "I'd love to take this off you." Then he held his breath while he waited for her to demand he get undressed first.

Her eyes sparkled instead. "Yes. Do it."

His breath left his lungs on a long, relief-filled sigh. He reached behind her, leaning into her, feeling the press of her breasts against his chest. He unhooked the bra but didn't immediately back away, even though he knew he had to in order to bare her breasts. Her scent wound around him. Her bare skin pressed against his. He lowered his head and rubbed his lips along the sensitive spot where it met her shoulder.

She moaned. "Tingly," she whispered. "Very tingly."

Rick leaned back only far enough to get rid of the bra, then dove in for another kiss. He didn't want her thinking too hard. He was certain she wanted to be doing something, not just standing there, taking what he was giving her. But as he touched her, he felt the surrender beneath the nerves. He never wanted to take away her independent spirit, but he wanted to show her that she didn't have to fight him all the time either.

He turned her around to face the window again. Her lovely breasts were small, but he slid his hands around her and cupped them, to prove to himself that they were each a perfect handful. Soft. Warm. He thumbed her nipples and savored the hiss that escaped her lips. Their gazes locked in the mirror and he continued tweaking one nipple while he slowly lowered the other hand to cup her mound again.

"I want to undress you," she whimpered even as she rocked against his hand. "I want my hands on you."

"I want that too. In a minute." He slipped his hand inside her panties and found her heat. "Just a minute." As he moved his fingers along her slick flesh, her eyes closed and her head dropped back against his shoulder. Right then, he wished he'd at least taken his shirt off so he could feel the slide of her soft hair against his skin.

"Open your eyes, sweetheart." Her eyes flew open and their gazes met again in the window. "Watch."

Rick seemed to be almost invisible in the glass. Eve's body practically glowed. Her pale skin was a stark contrast to his dark jeans and black T-shirt. Her golden hair shone against the black shirt as well.

"Look at you," he whispered. One of his hands still moved between her thighs. She'd spread them farther without him having to ask. His tanned arm stretched across her pale abdomen, his hand deep inside her white panties. "So pretty."

He still cupped one of her breasts with his other hand. He teased the nipple with his palm and her lips parted on a breathy gasp. He loved embracing her like this, pressing into her from behind and still being able to see her expression. To watch them in the glass and see his hands on her soft skin, watch her sweet body move in response to his touches.

Eve's breathing had become shallower as she moved her hips. He dipped a couple of fingers into her heated channel, so slippery with her arousal. Did she want him to keep going? Surely she'd stop him if it got to be too much, too intimate. She moaned but kept her eyes open and locked on his in the reflection. Her lips were parted. No smile, but no frown on her face either. Need. It was need he saw there.

He held her tighter against him as he tweaked her nipple and teased her slick flesh. Her hips rocked as she searched for the satisfaction he was offering her.

Rick couldn't deny her. The need was clear on her face, in the frantic movement of her body against him. Her ass rocked over his aching erection and he yearned to plunge into her, but he could wait. He wanted to give her what she needed first.

With two fingers still inside her, he flicked his thumb lightly over her clitoris, the bundle of nerves so hard and swollen. She quivered slightly, but when he brushed her clit harder with his thumb, she cried out his name and climaxed in his arms.

Somehow she kept her eyes open, still locked with his in the glass. Her body writhed in his embrace and he held her tight against him and kept niggling the button of nerves with his thumb to keep her flying.

Her knees must have weakened because she sank suddenly against him. He wrapped his arms around her, supporting her.

***

Eve couldn't believe Rick made her come while she just stood there and watched him do it. She could barely believe she'd let him.

It was almost as if it had been happening to someone else. Surreal, like viewing a faded movie scene. The woman arched gracefully, practically dancing on the arms of the handsome man. Her body naked, his completely clothed. Hers bucking, his motionless, except for one hand, surrounding her, supporting her. The other moving between her legs.

His fingers had called forth overwhelming sensations in her body. And the visual stimulation? It was the sexiest thing she'd ever experienced.

She gradually recovered from the incredible climax and her legs could hold her up again. The figures in the reflection in front of her came back into focus and she could think again. She was wearing nothing but her panties and Rick was still fully dressed. There was something very wrong about that. She turned away from the glass.

She slipped her hands beneath his shirt and sighed at the warm skin and hard muscles beneath her hands. She tugged at the hem. "Off. This needs to come off."

Rick chuckled and let her bare his brawny chest and strong shoulders, his broad back and muscular arms. Mmm. Obviously, working in construction and as a first responder kept him in great physical condition. And now she got to enjoy the benefits.

At least for tonight.

This was no time to think about how temporary their relationship would be. She slowly sank to her knees and reached for the button on the front of Rick's jeans. "My turn." She pressed her lips to his abs, the skin warm and tight. Then she kissed her way down to the waistband of his jeans. His breath caught when she took her kisses lower, along the fly, where he was hard and hot.

She finally slipped the button through its hole, then glanced up at Rick with a grin while she played with the metal tab of his zipper. Eve was certain he was as eager as she was for her to yank the zipper down and release his erection, but she wanted to take it slowly, like he had done with her.

Rick narrowed his eyes. Growled, actually growled at her. Oh yeah, he didn't want to go slow any longer. She laughed, feeling incredibly free. How did he make her feel so free? She dropped another kiss to the fly, felt the push of his arousal behind the denim. Eve pressed her cheek to his groin, soaking in his heat and the scent she knew as his. His hands dropped to her head and he pressed her tighter against him.

Eve glanced at the window and saw their reflections again. She was kneeling, naked, in front of Rick, her face in his crotch. What was she doing? Since her hand was on the tab, she yanked the zipper down, then shot to her feet. It was time to get away from that window, from the reflections she saw too clearly. "Didn't you say something about a bed?"

He grasped her hand and drew her down the hallway to the master bedroom. "This way. There's a bed in here, I promise."

He led her through the doorway and to the side of the king-sized bed. The nerves surprised her by coming back full force. After what they'd just done in front of the window, how could she be at all nervous? What could be more intimate than coming in a man's arms while she watched it happen?

Rick stepped out of his jeans and drew her onto the mattress. He knelt beside her, tangled his fingers in her hair and leaned in for a kiss. She thought she could smell the scent of her arousal on his hands, a reminder of how uninhibited she'd felt in his arms. He'd held her so close, so tight, yet she'd felt so free. He'd played with her body in all the right ways. She never thought it would be so hot to see herself there, completely naked while he was dressed and holding her that way. When he wouldn't let her drop her gaze, it was as if he was with her through every touch, every sensation. And she felt, just for a brief moment, as if they were one.

But they weren't one. Couldn't be. Not now. If she'd known this crazy attraction was going to raise its ugly head, she never would have approached Rick in the first place. Such lousy timing. This was *her* time. Her time to discover herself. To revel in her independence. No amount of sex could distract her from that.

But she could be enjoying the sex, enjoy being with Rick for a few more weeks. Speaking of sex...

Eve opened her arms.

Chapter Nine

Rick rolled over until he was on top of Eve, enjoying her smooth, bare body under his. Her eyes grew wide and so did her smile. The pale curves of her breasts called to him. He cupped the soft flesh in his hands while he buried his face between them. He breathed in her scent, tasted her on his lips. Her moan sang through the air and he promised himself to make her sing with pleasure often.

He ventured down her body until he reached her lacy underwear. He slid his fingers under the elastic and eased it over her hips. Once he'd tossed them away, he got rid of his briefs and then joined her once more in the center of the mattress, bare flesh to bare flesh.

Looking down on the sight she made in front of him, Rick let out a low sigh. "I know it hasn't been long since we had our first dinner together, but I feel like I've been waiting for this moment forever."

"The days have been long, haven't they?" Eve opened her arms wide. "Don't make me wait any longer. I want to feel you inside me."

"First..." He stretched out beside her on the bed and

bent his head to take one beaded nipple into his mouth, while he slid his hand down her body until he rested his hand between her thighs. “I want to make you feel good again.”

She frowned and pushed at his arm. “Oh no. I can’t. It’s your turn now.”

He didn’t lift his hand. “I want to watch you fly one more time.”

“No, Rick, I can’t do it. Don’t.”

He brushed his fingers along her slick flesh. “Are we going to argue about a second orgasm?”

She wriggled her hips. “I’ve never been able to have more than one at a time.”

“Really? Will it hurt to try?”

Eve looked up at him, her worried eyes wide, her lower lips between her teeth. “Um. I guess not.”

“Good.” Her tightly trimmed curls between her thighs glimmered with moisture. Rick slipped a finger along the slick flesh until he found the sensitive little bud that made her gasp. “So pretty. So sensitive. Don’t think about it, Eve. Just go with it.”

Her hips began to rock, her breath came faster, her moans louder. He loved feeling her soft body writhe beneath his hand. He slipped a couple of fingers into her core while he continued to use his thumb to tease her clit. He sucked harder on her nipple as he made love to her with his hand.

When her climax hit her, she arched off the bed. Her hands fisted the bedcovers and her eyes squeezed shut. Rick continued to stimulate her, letting her soar with her orgasm for a few more moments before gradually letting her come down.

“Wow,” she whispered.

“I knew you could do it.” He loved knowing he helped her do what she’d never been able to before.

He rolled to the side and grabbed a condom from

the drawer in his nightstand. While Eve's breathing slowed, he rolled it on and then stretched over her. Her eyes were wide, meeting his gaze with an unwavering look.

She grasped his hips and tugged. "Come on." She wrapped her legs around him and pressed her warmth against his erection. "Now, Rick. Now."

And when he slid into her, finally filled her, surrounded her, surrounded *by* her, he sighed with the overwhelming sense of belonging. She wrapped her arms around his back, her legs around his hips, and held on tightly. She met him thrust for thrust, breath for breath, sigh for sigh.

He caught his mouth with hers as his climax hit him. His groan of completion was lost in the kiss. He emptied into her, giving her everything he could. Then he almost collapsed on top of her, rolling to the side at the last minute so he didn't crush her.

She stared up at him, her eyes still slightly glazed. While he'd not really expected a wide smile on her face, the confused frown surprised him.

"You all right?" he asked.

***

She'd never been better. But should she admit it? Could she? How could she have had the best sex of her life and still feel like she shouldn't be this happy.

"I'm fine. You just wore me out." Eve snuggled against Rick, her head on his shoulder, her legs intertwined with his. They didn't say anything in a while, just stroked each other in this dark cozy cocoon. That was amazing. She couldn't believe she'd settled for mediocre sex all this time. She chuckled.

Rick's hand froze on her butt. "What?"

Did he think she'd laughed at him?

She patted his shoulder. "I was just thinking *poor Tiffany*. She's stuck with lousy sex with Don."

"Is that a compliment on my sex-in-a-bed skills?"

She couldn't help but laugh. "Ooh, your ego need a little stroking?"

The grin on his face told her he didn't need an ego boost. He knew he was good. While that should have ticked her off, it simply made him all the more attractive. A man who knew what a woman needed and knew how to give it to her. A confident man who didn't brag.

Eve knew she should head on home, but she sighed and rested her head back on his shoulder.

In a minute.

She must have dozed off because when the phone on his nightstand wailed, she jumped. Rick lunged out of bed.

"Sorry." He glanced at the text on his phone. "Fire alarm activation at one of the lake houses. I've got to go." He stepped into his underwear and grabbed a shirt with the Best Bay Volunteer Fire Department logo on the breast pocket.

"Be careful." She sat up. Her heart sped at the thought of Rick running into a burning building.

"Don't worry," he said as he stepped into his pants. "There's no visible smoke or flames. It's probably a false alarm." He sat on the side of the bed and pulled his shoes on. "Stay here." He leaned down and kissed her. "Get some sleep. I should be back soon."

Eve watched him dash out, then plopped back down on the mattress and snuggled into the covers. They smelled like Rick, a masculine scent that made her sigh and become aroused at the same time. Even though Rick invited her to stay, she knew she should go home. But she didn't want to leave this warm, soft, great-smelling bed.

She was comfortable. Happy. Rick said there was nothing to worry about. When he came back, maybe they could have more sex before they got some sleep. And then have breakfast together before they went to work.

She grabbed her cell phone off the nightstand on her side of the bed. She had to set her alarm a little earlier so she could meet Tess at her office before she opened the shop. Oh, and she'd promised to pick up coffee and muffins on the way. But that didn't mean she couldn't share breakfast with Rick. She adjusted the time on her alarm and set the phone back on the nightstand.

She wondered what he liked. She could fry up some eggs, or scramble them, if he preferred. Maybe he liked something heartier, like pancakes. She didn't care for them, they soaked up too much syrup but if he liked them—

Suddenly, Eve could barely breathe. No. No. What was she doing? She'd started to arrange her morning around Rick. She'd just escaped from mornings like that. She clambered out of bed and raced around, grabbing her clothes off the floor and dressing quickly. She had to get out of there before Rick came back.

She knew she was weak enough that she'd want to crawl back into bed with him if he came back before she was gone.

Once Eve was inside her house next door—the house that wouldn't be hers much longer—
she sank to the bottom tread on the stairs to catch her breath. She didn't turn on any lights. Let him think she came back here to get some sleep. How could anyone get any sleep with fire alarms going off at all hours of the night?

God, let it be a false alarm. She didn't like the thought of Rick rushing into a burning building. A couple of years ago her friend Bonnie's husband Frank had died fighting a fire in an old motel. The roof collapsed. Oh God. Her heart thudded when she thought how that could have happened to Rick. It could still happen to him.

How could she sleep until she knew he was home safe?

Eventually, she climbed the stairs to her bedroom. This had been her space since Donald left, since the kids moved out. Her little Eve-cave where she felt safe and secure. Where she was just *Eve* and not Mom or an ex-wife or a businesswoman. Generally, as soon as she entered the quiet space, she relaxed.

But tonight she couldn't unwind. She wished the apartment was finished and she was living in the center of the village, then she wouldn't be able to look out the window and know that Rick wasn't back from the fire call yet. How long was he likely to be gone if it was only a false alarm? Shouldn't he be back by now?

She loved living alone. She didn't have to justify to anyone if she didn't want to go to bed in the middle of the night. Didn't have to come up with a reason why she wasn't able to sleep. Why she paced the floor, picturing those big old lake houses and how quickly they could go up in flames.

She only sank into the chair by the window when she saw Rick's pick-up pull into his drive and disappear into his garage. What would he think if she stomped over to his house and demanded to know what took him so long? Didn't he know that people who cared about him wanted to get some sleep instead of worrying about flames and falling roofs?

Since she'd fled his house without leaving a note behind, he probably wouldn't be amused.

Eve reached for her phone to make an adjustment to the alarm, since she wouldn't be having breakfast with Rick, but it wasn't in her pocket. Or in between the chair and the cushion. It hadn't fallen to the floor either.

With a sinking stomach, she realized she'd left it on the nightstand in Rick's bedroom.

****

Eve was gone.

Disappointment crashed down on Rick. He was exhausted and had been looking forward to nothing more than spooning with Eve until morning. He stared at the empty bed. The sheets that still held her scent were tangled and bunched in the center of the mattress. She'd left his bed while he'd been out responding to a false alarm.

Who popped popcorn in the middle of the night? And then burned it? Fucking burnt popcorn was to blame for pulling him out of bed and giving Eve an opportunity to escape.

Why did she want to leave? He thought everything had been going well. The sex had been amazing. But she didn't even leave a note.

Maybe he'd pushed too hard. That crazy sexy stuff in front of the window hadn't been planned but she'd inspired it. She'd been all in at the time, he was certain of it. So something happened after he left on the call to make her run away.

Was that why she fled? She didn't like that he'd left her alone in bed while he went out on a fire call? She'd have to get used to that. He was going to respond when he was needed. If she couldn't deal with that, they'd never have a future together. Still, Rick had never thought Eve would be the kind of woman to resent his responsibilities to the community.

He slowly undressed. His poor body had no problem complaining when he dragged it out of bed in the middle of the night. His knees ached tonight. He was in better shape than a lot of the other guys, but he was still fifty-five.

What business did he have playing around with Eve as if they were young kids? Once she had time to think about it, she probably thought the whole night was too kinky for her. Hell, he'd never considered himself unconventional. He wouldn't blame her for being freaked out except...man, watching Eve ride out her orgasm in his arms in the reflection in the glass was the hottest thing he'd ever seen. He wouldn't have wanted to miss that. The thing was, he could have sworn she wouldn't have wanted to miss it either.

Maybe he didn't know her as well as he thought he did.

He had half a mind to go over there right now and demand to know what had happened. But her house was dark. She must be asleep already. The morning would be soon enough to talk to her. And a glance at his clock told him that morning wasn't too many hours away.

Rick had just rested his head on the pillow when his doorbell rang. His heart raced. Eve? Had she changed her mind?

He tugged a pair of shorts on and hurried down the hall. He flung open the door to find her standing there in the same clothes she'd worn earlier. The look of chagrin on her face told him she wasn't angry at him. Then what had happened?

"You didn't even leave a note." He hadn't moved away from the doorway. Didn't let her in. He was more hurt than he realized by her escape.

She stood on the stoop and crossed her arms. Her gaze bounced all around. "I know. I'm sorry. That was wrong of me."

"Why did you come back?" He wanted her to tell him that there had been an emergency. Or that she'd made a mistake and she was sorry.

She cleared her throat. "I forgot my phone."

"What?" She hadn't come back to him? She'd only come back for her cell phone?

"I left my phone on the nightstand."

"Get it then," he snapped. He stepped back and gestured her inside with an exaggerated flourish.

"Rick, don't." She stepped into the foyer and he closed the door.

He followed her into the bedroom. He took her arm because he had to touch her again. "What's going on, Eve? Why did you leave?"

She wouldn't look at him. She stared at the stupid phone in her hand. "I have to get up early to meet with Tess. I didn't want to wake you."

"That's not why." He tugged her back to look at him. "Don't lie to me, Eve. I thought we were past the games. We have to be honest with each other."

She yanked her arm away and stalked across the room. "This wasn't supposed to happen." She whirled around to glare at him. "I don't want to like you so much."

Rick worked hard to match her intense expression when he simply wanted to smile. "I like you too."

"I don't want my life to revolve around you."

"I never asked you for that." But he could see his life revolving around her.

"I know. It's not your fault."

"Don't you dare give me the *It's not you, it's me* crap."

"But it's the truth. You want more than I can give right now."

"All I asked is to give things a try until the wedding. Is that so hard? I haven't asked you to move in with me. I haven't asked for a life-long commitment. Did I push you too much tonight? Was the sex too much?"

"God, no. The sex...the sex was amazing."

"Then what's the problem?"

"Sex isn't everything. Okay, it's a big thing, but it isn't everything."

"So did I push you too much? Am I pushing you too much?"

"No. I don't think so. No, you didn't."

"Tell me what you're thinking, Eve. I'm going crazy here trying to figure out what to do. Or what not to do."

"I got scared, okay? Scared I'm going to fall into the same life I had with Don. And at the time, I didn't even know it was a bad life. It wasn't a bad life for the most part. But it's not the life I want anymore."

"What kind of life do you want now?"

"A life of my own. A life *on* my own. I know that sounds selfish, but I don't want to have to pick up after anyone but myself. I don't want to worry about what someone else wants for breakfast. Or dinner. I love to entertain but I want to invite people I like, not law partners and clients and pretty young interns."

"Okay, well, I don't have any law partners or interns. I like to eat practically anything and I can pick up after myself."

Her lower lip jutted out into an almost-pout. "Now you're being sensible."

Rick smiled. "I usually am." He opened his arms and this time she walked into them. He folded her into his embrace and hoped he'd calmed her fears, at least for tonight. He hoped Eve would find a way to have the life she needed and still choose to include him.

Chapter Ten

It had been a busy Saturday morning, and when Eve locked the door to her shop at noon, she was glad she hadn't had too much time to be nervous about going with Rick to his daughter's home for a cook-out. It was crazy to be nervous around Heather. She'd spent as much time at the Corcoran house as Amy had at the Best's. Eve was glad that the girls were still good friends, even though they were both grown now with lives of their own. The nerves weren't really for Heather herself, but for the expectations she might have because she thought Eve was dating her father.

Eve carried a big bowl of salad into the kitchen of the charming bungalow where Heather lived with her policeman husband, Ryan. Heather squealed when she saw Eve, just like she used to do when she was a little girl.

"Mrs. C., you're here!" Heather grabbed the salad bowl and placed it on the counter, then threw her arms around Eve. "I'm so glad to see you."

"She just wants your salad."

Eve turned and grinned at Amy. "Hey, sweetie." She

gave her daughter a hug and then turned back to Heather. "You know I can give you the recipe."

"I think you already did. But it always tastes so much better when you make it." Heather looked over Eve's shoulder. "Where's my dad?"

"I think he took his cooler to the back yard."

"Oh, he didn't have to bring beer. Ryan made sure we had plenty."

"He said something about hating to run out," Eve told her.

"Guys and their beer." Heather stowed the salad bowl in the refrigerator.

"I could use one," Amy said. "Come on, Mom. Let's go out back. I'm thirsty."

Eve turned to Heather. "Anything I can do to help first?"

"My duties are done," Heather told her. "The rest is up to the guys and the grill. I'm coming out too."

There were five handsome men gathered around the big blue beer cooler. Along with Rick, Heather's husband Ryan and Amy's fiancé Blake, Rick's two brothers, Max and John were there.

"Hope you haven't finished all that beer yet," Heather called out. The guys just laughed. She turned to Eve. "There's water and wine coolers too."

Eve glanced at Rick and he lifted a brow in a silent inquiry. "I'll start with a beer. Might change to water later." He grabbed a drink for her and she followed Rick to a bench underneath a maple tree. He handed her the can. "Thanks." They sat there a moment and Eve watched the kids interacting. "Isn't it kinda weird watching our kids acting like adults?"

Rick looked at her. "They *are* adults."

"I know. But to me they'll always be our kids."

"That's what my mom says. We may be in our forties and fifties, but we're still her kids. That's why she thinks she can still interfere. Of course, she doesn't consider it interfering."

Eve chuckled. "Of course not."

The sun beat down, but there was a nice breeze where they sat in the shade of the maple. "God, I'm feeling my age," Rick grumbled. "It used to be us running around taking care of all the details. Remember, when we'd have cookouts in our backyards?"

Somedays it seemed like yesterday and sometimes it felt like a million years ago. "Now we're the old folks sitting back, taking it easy."

"I don't want to be one of the old folks yet." Rick set his beer can on the ground beneath the bench.

Eve agreed. "We're as young as we feel, isn't that the saying?"

"And I feel like doing something besides sitting here like a bump on a log." He grabbed her hand and pulled her to her feet. "Come on."

Eve set her can on the bench before she followed him across the yard. Rick picked up a blue Frisbee lying in the grass by the fence and tossed it her way. She laughed and caught it, tossed it back. It had been years since she'd played like this. Soon the rest of the group joined in and they all worked up an appetite before sitting down to plates of burgers and salad and slices of sweet watermelon.

Rick had taken only a couple of bites of burger when alarms rang from the phones of all three Best brothers. The groans travelled down the table.

"Figures," John said. "I swear we get more calls at meal time than any other."

Max nodded as he shoved the rest of his burger into his mouth and climbed off the picnic table bench.

"Good thing I only had that half a beer." Rick looked up from the message on his phone. "EMS.

Shelley's on the board." He sent Eve an apologetic smile and gestured to his plate. "Can you wrap that up for me? I'll finish it when I get back." He dropped a kiss to the top of her head. "Have fun with the kiddos."

He and his brothers piled into his truck and took off for the fire hall.

"Not often I can sit back and not respond to an emergency situation," Ryan said. He took another bite of burger, obviously quite pleased that he had the day off and didn't have to walk away from his meal.

Amy narrowed her eyes as she looked at Heather. "You're drinking water?"

Heather shrugged. "Yeah? Felt like water today."

Amy leaped up, almost knocking over her plate. "You're pregnant? Oh my God, you guys are pregnant!"

Ryan's eyes went wide. "What?"

"Easy," Heather said with a laugh. Her cheeks turned pink. "We're not pregnant. But we *are* trying."

"I knew it! I knew there was some reason you didn't have a beer in your hand." Amy sat back down on at the table and picked up her burger.

"I don't drink beer that often."

"At a cook-out? With burgers? Yeah, you do. Ever since you were old enough to drink legally." Amy nudged her. "And sometimes before that."

Heather protested loudly. Blake and Ryan shook their heads and laughed, then started to debate the chances of the Bills having a winning football season. Amy and Heather started discussing the upcoming bachelorette party. Eve ate her meal and just enjoyed listening to the kids talk. But in the back of her mind, she couldn't help but wonder if Rick was driving the ambulance again, or lifting a stretcher, or perhaps performing some kind of life-saving procedure.

She knew it took a certain type of person to be willing to jump into any emergency situation, willing to help the members of a community in times of trouble. No matter the trouble. No matter the danger.

Even though it scared her a little, she knew Rick wouldn't be any other way. And she admired that about him.

When they were finished eating, Eve helped the girls carry everything into the kitchen. She covered Rick's plate and placed it in the refrigerator while Amy and Heather continued their wedding conversation.

Amy was a whirlwind as she helped Heather put things away. "Mom, have you found your dress yet?" she called over her shoulder.

"Not yet."

"You don't have much time left."

"I have plenty of time. I didn't find anything I liked locally. Maybe I'll get Maggie and Tess to go shopping in Erie with me. Maybe next weekend. Or the weekend after."

"Don't wait too long."

"I won't, sweetie. I just want to find something attractive." Before when Eve had shopped for a dress to wear to the wedding, all she'd worried about was not looking drab and old-fashioned. Now all she could think about was finding something that would put a spark in Rick's eyes when he saw her in it. "You know...hot."

"No. No. No." Amy looked as horrified as if Eve had told her she was going to march down the aisle naked. "The mother of the bride is not supposed to look hot. She's supposed to look like a mother. The bride's mother."

Eve didn't expect the hurt that speared her chest. Her daughter didn't consider her a woman. She was only a mother. "Dowdy."

Heather jumped in to Amy's defense, "Not dowdy, Mrs. C., you could never look like that no matter what you're wearing. But the mother of the bride's not supposed to look, you know, sexy." Heather winced. "Sorry."

Eve laughed and hoped it didn't sound too forced. She kissed Amy's cheek. "Sweetie, don't worry. Your old mother wasn't planning on sexy." Though she'd like Rick to think she was.

"I'm sorry, Mom. You're not old. I don't mean that. There's just a certain way the mother of the bride is supposed to look. It's like, tradition."

Eve pasted a smile on her face. "Well, it's your wedding. If you want a frumpy looking mother in all your photos, I'm sure I can find any number of dresses that fit that bill. But I am disappointed you'd want your mom to feel unattractive."

"That's not what I mean, Mom."

"I know." But it was the way it sounded to Eve. Was that why bridal shops stocked unattractive, matronly looking dresses? Tradition? She might just have to buck tradition. "Don't worry. There's no way I would embarrass the bride." Eve turned around and stalked out the door.

Amy and Heather followed her outside, apologizing the whole way. Eve ignored them. She'd had enough of that conversation. Women of a certain age seemed to be expected to take a back seat to the rest of the world. Stay invisible and don't draw attention to themselves. She certainly didn't want to upstage the bride, but what was wrong with wanting to look attractive?

It was time to change the subject. "The guys aren't back yet? What could be taking them so long?" They sat back down at the picnic table.

"It usually takes them at least an hour on a rescue call," Heather told her. "Depending on what the problem is, of course. But by the time they respond, stabilize the victim, transport them to the hospital and then get back to the hall, yeah, I remember it was usually about an hour minimum."

"Okay, I guess I—" Eve stopped when she saw an elderly couple, arms linked, walk around the house and into the back yard. It had been a while since she'd seen Rick's parents, but she recognized them instantly. "Hello."

Heather jumped up. "Gram? Gramps? I thought you were visiting Uncle Pete today."

"He has a cold. A nasty summer cold. Summer colds are terrible." Martha Best crossed the yard slowly, the breeze catching the bright pink shirt she wore over white pants. "So we decided to visit our granddaughter instead."

"I'm glad you did." Heather hurried over to help her grandmother across the uneven ground.

"Looks like a party going on." Ted Best, a tall and thin elder version of Rick, glanced over to Eve and winked. His knobby knees stood out between his khaki shorts and leather sandals. "Nice to see you, dear." Then he turned to Ryan and held out his hand.

"Good to see you, sir." Ryan shook his hand. "Not a party. Just burgers and beer."

Martha kissed Heather on the cheek and then turned to Eve and threw her arms wide. "Eve! I'm so glad to see you!"

"Hello, Martha." Rick's mother wrapped her up in a big hug. Eve sank into her softness and then pulled gently away before she sneezed from an overdose of honeysuckle perfume. A wave of nostalgia came over her. Her mother used to wear that scent.

"I'm so happy to hear you and Rick are dating. Where is my oldest son?" Martha looked around as if she thought he was hiding behind the broad maple tree.

"Rescue call," Heather told her. "Should be back soon."

Ryan pulled a couple of burgers from the warming

rack on the grill. "Hungry? We have plenty."

"No, no. Thanks," Ted said. "We ate before we came over." He joined Ryan and Blake over by the grill.

"But I wouldn't mind a bite of dessert if you have any," Martha said.

"Gram, I think you must be who I get my sweet tooth from," Heather said with a smile. "I was going to wait until Dad and Uncle Max and Uncle John got back, but I can cut the ice cream sandwich cake now if you want some."

Martha sat on the bench where Eve and Rick had been sitting earlier. "No, dear. We can wait." Eve couldn't miss the speculative gleam in Martha's eye before she patted the bench next to her. "Come sit beside me, Eve."

Terror. Sheer terror. Martha was going to want to talk about her and Rick. Was she going to have to lie to Rick's mother? Somehow, she had a feeling Martha wouldn't take everything at face value like their kids did.

How long before she could come up with an excuse and escape? She'd have to wait for Rick. She knew they should have driven separately. This was just what she didn't want – pointed questions from his mother. Eve almost pled a call of nature and escaped to the house never to return. Instead, her ingrained manners had her smiling and taking a seat beside Martha.

"It's a lovely day, isn't it?" Eve commented. Anything to not talk about her and Rick.

"It's a beautiful day," Martha replied, then took Eve's hand. "You knew Rick's wife, Cathy."

"Yes, of course. We lived next door to each other. We were friends."

"She was a wonderful woman and..."

Eve knew she shouldn't prompt Rick's mother, but she couldn't help it. "And?"

"And Rick loved her so much." Tears glittered in Martha's eyes. "But I've been so worried that he would never let himself love someone again."

Love? No, they couldn't talk about love. "Oh, well..."

"I don't want my sons to be lonely, Eve. You understand that, I'm sure. Men aren't made to live all alone. I'm so glad he found you."

"Martha, we've only just started dating."

"All relationships have to start with the first date, don't they?"

"I just don't want you to expect..."

Martha patted her hand. "Don't worry. I'm not expecting anything, dear. Hoping. I'm hoping my son will be happy with you. That's all." Martha glanced over to where Amy and Heather were talking together by the picnic table. "How are the wedding plans coming?"

"Good," Eve replied. "Everything's done, I think."

"You don't have a dress yet," Amy chimed in.

Her daughter wasn't going to let her forget it. "I still have time."

Martha sighed. "I hope I get the chance to celebrate a few more weddings while I still have time."

Eve didn't want another wedding. She didn't want a marriage like her parents had. She didn't want a marriage like she had with Don. She glanced around the backyard. The men were on the other side talking about whatever men talked about when they went off by themselves at these kinds of gatherings.

Just then she heard Rick's truck pull in and the doors slam. Eve sighed with relief. He was back. A buffer between her and Martha. A voice of reason after all this talk of weddings. A ride home.

Martha called out. "Max. John. Come over here." Rick followed his brothers into the backyard. "You see this lovely woman here? This is your brother's girlfriend. You know what a girlfriend is, don't you?"

Eve felt her cheeks heat.

Martha shook her finger at her grown sons as if they were children again. "Man was not meant to live alone." She threw her arm around Eve's shoulder. "It's not right. You boys should all be married."

Rick grimaced. "Mom, enough with the married talk."

"Leave the kids alone, Martha," Ted said, then turned back to his conversation with Ryan and Blake.

"I tried it once already, Mom," John shot back. "Not cut out to be a husband."

"Still haven't found the right woman," Max added and then headed for the grill, probably looking for an excuse to escape. If only Eve could think of one.

"If you boys are not married before I die, I will haunt you until you are."

Rick shook his head and caught Eve's gaze with an apologetic glance. "Mom..."

"I just want my boys to be happy."

"I'm happy," Max told her with a big grin, another burger in his hand.

John nodded. "Me too."

"Well, at least my Ricky has found someone."

No. No. No. Eve pulled away from Martha and jumped to her feet. "I have to go. Um, Rick, I need to go home. Now." Everyone was staring at her. Could someone actually pass out from embarrassment? "Um, dog. I have to let the dog out."

"When did you get a dog?" Amy asked.

Her face burned. They hadn't had a dog in years, but it had been her go-to excuse whenever she wanted to leave a function early. "I didn't. I don't know what I'm saying. I'm tired." She turned to Rick. If only she'd taken her own car, she could have slipped off and not had to come up with a really bad excuse so she could get a ride home. "I'm sorry. I'm exhausted. I didn't sleep much last night."

Rick was at her side in a moment and took her hand. "No problem. Bye, guys. Thanks for the party. Sorry we had to bug out for a while, but Little League practice got a little rough and one of the kids broke their arm." He smiled at her. "Let's go."

"Oh, wait. Your dinner. You didn't get a chance to eat." She was being selfish, pulling him away just because his mother was freaking her out. He'd want to stay to eat. He should be able to stay and eat. Visit with his parents. "We can stay a while longer. Eat first."

He put his arm around her waist. "I've got food at home."

"I'll grab your plate." Heather put her words into action, ran into the house, and came back out with the covered plate.

Eve took it. "Thanks for inviting me."

Rick kept his arm around her all the way to the truck. Eve felt the eyes of everyone on them as they walked away.

As soon as they were in his truck, Eve turned to Rick. "I'm sorry, but that was too real. I just need a wedding date, not a relationship. I'm not ready for that much commitment. I may never be."

"Okay," he said with no hesitation at all. "Whatever you want."

Eve knew she should have felt relief, but all she felt was sad.

***

Rick knew his mom could be relentless. She must have been pushing Eve for a while before he and his brothers got back from the call. Now Eve was all skittish again. Back to insisting there was no chance for them. What could he do but agree with her? He'd lose her right now if he tried to fight her on it. Even though he knew there was no way they could walk away from each other in a few weeks. Didn't Eve know that?

All he could do right now was try to reassure her. "I'm sorry about my Mom. I know she's pushy. She means well, but she doesn't have much of a filter."

Eve spun in her seat. "I can't do it. I can't risk falling back into the life I had before."

And here's where he'd love to try to reason with her, tell her that life with him wouldn't be the same as living with Don, but why would she believe him? He started the truck. "If you still feel this way the day after the wedding, I'll tell everyone you broke it off, so Donald can't turn it back around on you." Even as Rick said it, he hoped to hell they never got to that point.

"Thank you." With a sigh, Eve fastened her belt and gripped the plate with his dinner on it as he pulled out of the drive. "I promise to play the part until the wedding. I'll hold your hand and smile into your eyes and introduce you to everyone as my boyfriend."

"No. I told you, not boyfriend." It still sent an embarrassing twist to his stomach every time he heard it. He couldn't help but picture his old kindergarten teacher in her underwear. "Don't call me that."

"I don't understand. Why not?"

"A fifty-five year old man is not a *boy*friend."

"Your mother called me your *girl*friend." The corner of her lip quirked. "What do you want me to call you, *man*friend?"

"That sounds stupid too."

"Special friend? Lover? My guy? Come on, give me some help here. Or should we just forget the whole thing."

Panic spiked. He needed time, needed all the weeks they had left to convince her to change her mind. "Friend? Isn't friend okay?" He glanced over to see her shrug. "I have a feeling everyone around here already figures we're lovers, so I doubt there will be many introductions needed."

"Well, we are. Aren't we?" Her voice took on that slow, sexy tone he didn't hear nearly enough.

"Friends? Yeah, we're friends."

"I know we are, but I was talking about lovers. We are lovers, aren't we? Or does only one time not count?"

He wanted to laugh with joy. He'd been afraid her taking their relationship back to square one meant that sex was off the table now.

"Oh, it counts." He turned into his driveway and pulled into the garage. As soon as the door went down behind them, he reached out and drew her close, as close as she could be with the console in between them. He locked her gaze with his. "But that doesn't matter because it's not going to be only the one time."

"It's not?"

"Of course not."

She slid her fingers in his hair and brought his mouth to hers with a painful tug. "Good." She dragged her tongue along his lips and he opened eagerly to her demand.

His stomach growled, interrupting the hot, wet kiss. "Hey you're not going to dump my dinner on the floor of my truck, are you?"

"I wouldn't think of it." She turned around and set the plate on the floor behind her seat. "There. Safe." Then she got up on her knees in her seat and stretched over the console as she wrapped her arms around his neck and caught his mouth again.

Sweet. So sweet. He never got over how delicious she tasted. Or how the shivery moans she made vibrated right through him. He cradled her head in his hands. Not to hold her in place but to support her as she roamed her mouth over him.

"We could go inside, you know," he murmured.

"In a minute."

He tipped his head to the side when she ran her warm slick lips along his jaw and then dipped her mouth into the sensitive juncture of his neck and shoulder. “God, Eve.” He understood now why this used to be called *necking*.

She swatted at him, but chuckled. “I’m not used to being so out of control. I don’t know if I like it.”

“You love it.”

“Maybe.”

He was already hard and hurting, but because she had pled exhaustion he had to ask, “So how tired are you?”

Her eyes sparkled. “I’ve gotten my second wind.”

“You don’t know how glad I am to hear that.” He shot her a smile and shut off the engine. “Come on inside and I’ll let you take control.” That’s what she wanted, wasn’t it?

“Really? I can do whatever I want?”

“You can even tell me what to do.”

“Deal.”

Chapter Eleven

The next couple of weeks flew by. When Eve decided to sell the house, she hadn't realized the incredible amount of work there would be in sorting through twenty-five years' worth of papers, mementos, and everyday stuff. She was down-sizing in a big way but it wasn't just her things she had to deal with, but what was left of Amy's and Seth's and Don's too. Most evenings she spent sorting through the closets and cabinets. Tonight she climbed the stairs to the attic to see what was up there.

God, it was hot up there. And dusty. Cobwebby. There wasn't as much up there as she thought. Just a row of blue plastic totes along the wall. When was the last time she'd opened one, or even needed to come up here to look for something? She couldn't remember, which meant it had been years.

She pulled off the top of the first tote and saw it was filled with spare blankets she'd forgotten all about. Donate. Several more were crammed with kids' clothes, outgrown years ago. Donate. The last one was full of VHS tapes. Really? She scanned the ones on top. Cartoons. Superheroes. Disney princesses. She sighed and sat down on the dusty wood floor. When the kids were little, they had family movie night every Friday night. It had been a big treat for the kids to each pick out a movie to watch. Don had always been home in time. He loved the movies as much as the kids.

Then the kids grew older and wanted to do things with friends on Friday night. Don started working late more often. VHS gave way to DVDs. Then streaming.

Their family had changed as much, and as quickly, as did the methods of movie viewing.

Eve shoved the lid back on the tote. She'd donate the tapes, but did anyone even own a VHS player anymore?

It was already August. Seth would be here in a couple of weeks. One moment she wanted to move into the apartment as soon as possible. But then she sank into the bedroom chair at the end of the day and told herself she should wait until after the wedding. Didn't she have enough going on this month? Labor Day weekend would be there before she knew it and she didn't even have a dress yet.

Oh God. She had to shop for a dress before the wedding.

She and Rick made it a point to go out to eat a couple of evenings and the community seemed to have accepted them as a couple with no awkward questions or exclamations of disbelief. They'd made love on those evenings as well and Eve kept it to herself that she missed him when they weren't together.

She told herself she was too busy to be lonely.

It didn't matter. She was strong enough now. Stronger than her mother had been. Stronger than she herself had been when she jumped into marriage straight out of college. She could resist Rick Best. She could embrace her independence. Embrace a life on her own.

He'd kept her up to date with the progress on her apartment and she'd been pleasantly surprised by how quickly they were finishing the renovations. The steam shower had finally come in and it was being installed this week. The pink tiles had already been painted a soft cream. The small pantry and the closet on the landing were finished and looked as if they'd been there all along. Max had designed an amazing amount of storage in a smaller-than-average bedroom closet. All that was left was refinishing the kitchen floor. She could move in this weekend if she had furniture.

Oh God. She had to shop for furniture before she could move in.

The cell phone in her pocket vibrated. She pulled it out and saw that it was Rick and couldn't help but smile. "Hey there."

"Hey yourself. Do I see lights up in the attic tonight?"

"It had to be done. It's a dirty job but someone...you know how it goes."

"Need some help?"

"Thanks, but I think I'm done up here. In fact, I think I've seen enough boxes and totes for tonight. So let me ask you something."

"Sure."

"How'd you like to have a movie night?"

He laughed. "What are we watching?"

"We each get to pick a movie. Bring over a DVD or I have streaming." She hadn't watched a movie in months. At the moment it sounded like the best idea in the world.

"Have you eaten? I can order a pizza."

"And I can pop some popcorn."

"Okay, but don't burn it."

***

It took Rick a moment to figure out where he was when he woke up the next morning. His neck had a crick in it, the sunlight was streaming in from the wrong direction, and a soft-scented weight was pressed into his lap. A smile broke out before he even opened his eyes.

Of course, he was in Eve's living room, curled up on the sofa with her blonde head on his lap. They'd laughed their way through a quirky comedy, but he barely remembered the start of the second movie. Evidently Eve had fallen asleep at some point as well.

They'd had a fun, relaxing evening. Chowing on pepperoni pizza, munching on popcorn and finishing a bottle of wine. No wonder they'd nodded off.

Rick shifted. Eve's head was pressing on his bladder and while he loved holding her close, he had to get up. "Eve."

She mumbled and snuggled deeper into him.

"Eve," he said a little louder. She turned over and he was able to slide out from under her and headed to the bathroom. On his way back to the living room, he checked the time. "Hey, Eve, what time do you need to get up for work."

She blinked her eyes as she looked up at him. "Rick?"

He grinned. "Good morning." She looked adorable with sleep-tousled hair, squinting up at him. "It's seven thirty. You open at nine, right?"

Eve groaned and flipped over. "Isn't it Sunday?"

He couldn't stop grinning. "Nope. Tuesday."

She groaned again. "What are you so happy about?"

"I don't know. We spent the night together and didn't even have sex. And yet I'm smiling."

"Amazing." Eve threw an arm over her eyes.

"I never knew you weren't a morning person."

"Be quiet. Don't sound so chipper." But she pushed herself to her feet and shuffled into the bathroom.

"You need to get a more comfortable couch," Rick called out when he heard her open the door.

"Why? Are you planning on sleeping on it again?"

He rubbed his neck. "You never know. But you're right, it will be more important for the bed to be comfortable." He pulled her into his arms. "Think we have time to go upstairs and check it out before we leave?"

"No time." She sounded irritated, but she melted against him. "I don't sleep on it anyway."

"What do you mean?"

"I think Don might have *entertained* Tiffany there. I haven't slept in that bed since I found out about the affair."

"You bought a new one for the apartment then?"

"I will. I just haven't gotten around to it yet."

"I thought you wanted to move in this weekend."

"I've been packing. Sorting. Working. Spending time with you. Haven't had time."

"Let's go tonight after work."

"You want to go with me to pick out furniture? I can do it myself. It's my apartment. My furniture. I really don't need any help with that."

"I know you don't," he said through gritted teeth. "But I thought it might be more fun to have someone with. Besides, I want to make sure the bed is comfortable. I plan on being there often."

She narrowed her eyes. "Only three more weeks until the wedding."

So she kept reminding him. "No more sex after the wedding?"

"Rick, we agreed."

He pulled her closer, brushed his lips along her throat. Slid his hands down to cup her bottom and lift her up to rub against his erection. "You won't miss the sex?"

"Yes." The word sounded as if it was pulled out of her. "But I can't deal with all the expectations. Not yours so much as everyone else's. God, everyone acts as if we're going to be getting married next."

"And you sure don't want to get married," he ground out.

"Of course not," she laughed, oblivious to Rick's distress. "I know you get it, but no one else does. It'll be so much easier once we can say we've broken up."

It didn't sound easy at all to Rick.

***

They popped into the BB&G for a quick dinner before heading out to look at furniture. Eve had all her measurements and had worked up as much excitement for the shopping as she had an appetite for a BB&G burger. She and Rick discussed what she was looking for while they ate.

When they were nearly finished, a group of men came in together and took the table next to them. She recognized two of them as Rick's brothers, Max and John. They all started throwing them looks and asked Eve what she was doing with Rick.

He rolled his eyes. "What are you guys doing here?"

Eve realized they were all members of the volunteer fire department. Or did they work for Best Brothers? Maybe it was a little of both.

"Same as you, I'd guess," Ben Krasinski said. "I'm here for the food." He was a lean and wiry guy with silver hair. He owned the local service station, so she knew he didn't work construction. But she was pretty sure he was in the fire department. She couldn't pull her eyes away from the full sleeves of tattoos he wore on both his arms. Sexy.

"Guess you forgot it was Tuesday night?" Joe Waterman said with a laugh. Joe was a nice guy who'd retired from professional firefighting. Evidently he couldn't get enough and volunteered now. Rick had mentioned Joe helped BBBuilders out when they needed an extra hand. “A pretty lady like this would have me losing my mind too.”

Rick glanced at Eve. “Yeah. Tuesday. A bunch of us usually stop here on Tuesday nights before drill.”

“Drill?” she asked.

“We practice going into a burning building or do maintenance on equipment. Things like that,” he explained. “Once a week.” He turned to look at the other firemen. “Yeah, guess I didn’t think what day it was. Listen, I’m going to miss drill tonight.”

“Hose test?” Ben sent him a frown. “You’re bailing on hose test?”

“You never miss drill,” John chimed in.

“I don’t blame him,” Max said, winking at Eve. “Rick’s probably rolled more hose than anyone else in the department. Give him a break, guys.”

Rick lifted a brow at his brother. “You’re being too nice. What do you want?”

“I’ll think of something. We’ll give the chief your regrets.”

“Excuses, you mean,” Ben grumbled.

Rick pushed his plate away. “I’m stuffed, sweetheart. How about you?”

“Yeah, I’m ready to go.” To keep up their charade, Eve took his hand as they left. It felt right, way too right for her hand to be cradled in his. Why? Why did she have to fall for this man now? Now that she was learning to be on her own? Getting stronger. Happier.

This was her time to find *herself*. Why did she have to find Rick now?

He was a great person to bounce off ideas. He pointed out the perfect table, dark and square, with four chairs to set in front of the new window in the kitchen. She found a deep green upholstered sofa and two chairs for the living room. Rick checked out the sofa for comfort before Eve told the salesman to add it to the order. Simple. The bed on the other hand...

He pulled her down on the fourth sample mattress. They lay on their backs, side by side. "What do you think of this one, sweetheart?"

"It feels the same as the last one."

Rick rolled on his side to look at her. "No. This one's firmer."

"If you say so." She rolled on her side to face at him. "I think the first one was the most comfortable."

"But how do you know if you don't test out the rest of them? The next one could end up being the most comfortable. Or even the very last one."

She laughed. "You just want to get me on as many beds in one night as you can."

He leaned in and kissed her. "You've uncovered my dastardly plan."

"If your fellow firefighters could see you now."

He put his arm around her waist and pulled her close before he kissed her again. "They would all be jealous."

"Any questions?" The salesman, a young man around Seth's age, stood over them, looking slightly embarrassed. He probably thought people their age shouldn't be indulging in PDAs. But that had been part of the agreement.

Of course, until now their agreement had been the last thing on her mind. Eve smiled up at the salesman. "No, thanks. Just trying out the mattresses. For comfort." The quirk of the salesman's lips made her want to giggle.

"Of course. Let me know when you've decided. I'm putting your order together now."

"Thank you." As soon as he walked away, Eve turned into Rick and laughed. He wrapped his arms around her and laughed too.

"My God, Eve. What are you doing?"

She knew that booming voice. She resisted the urge to jump away, as if she'd been caught doing something sinful. They weren't doing anything wrong. Eve looked up from Rick's shoulder. Her ex-husband and his new wife stared and she wanted to laugh again. "Hello, Donald. We're testing mattresses. What are you doing?"

"Why do you insist on giving the rumor mills more to talk about?" he demanded, as if the entire population of Best Bay was gathered in the memory foam mattress section, watching.

There were so many ways she could respond to that. Like didn't he realize what the village rumor mills had churned out when he took up with a woman younger than his daughter? Like he didn't have any business commenting on her actions. Like what did he care because anything she did wouldn't reflect on his lawyerly reputation anymore anyway? But in the end she sat up and told him the only thing that mattered.

"I really don't care what anyone else thinks. Including you." She gave Rick another quick kiss. "I like the first mattress. Let's go with that."

Rick got up and held out his hand. She let him help her to her feet and turned her back on Don and Tiffany. She walked away, her hand in Rick's, to get on with her new life.

It felt pretty damn good.

***

It had taken all the control Rick had to stop from jumping off that mattress, getting in Don Corcoran's face and telling him to leave Eve alone if he knew what was good for him. Hell, Don was the one who'd left her and he had no business demanding anything of her now.

But Rick knew how important it was for Eve to deal with her ex-husband on her own. As much as he'd wanted to leap in to help her, he'd been proud of the way she stood up to Don and then turned her back on him without causing a big scene. Don and Tiffany must have left the store after that because they didn't run into them again while they finished shopping.

The furniture would be delivered that weekend and she was as excited as a young woman getting her first place of her own. And then Rick remembered.

Eve *was* getting her first place of her own.

"I think we should celebrate," he told her.

She turned into his arms in the parking lot. "Ooh, what should we do to celebrate?" She took his mouth in a hard kiss. "Soon I'll be able to say *my place or yours*."

He chuckled. "Sex will be good but first I was thinking about ice cream."

Eve leaned back to look him in the face, a skeptical gleam in her eye. "Really? I thought sex was the first thing on any guy's mind."

"Oh, it is, but you've been talking about hitting The Shed for days now." The Ice Cream Shed was a favorite summer spot down by the beach and he wanted to show Eve he wasn't always about getting her into bed. "I'll park at your place and we can walk down for a cone." Beach-side parking was at a premium in the summer.

"Great idea."

As they walked the couple of blocks to the beach, Rick knew that in a few short weeks, Eve had become more important to him that he'd ever expected. He didn't want to be alone anymore. And he didn't want any other woman beside him.

Would she freak out if she knew he was falling in love with her? He was certain she would. But Rick thought back to a rescue call he'd responded to the day before. Bob Furlow, a fifty-year old friend of his brother, Max, who'd never reported having chest pains before, died of a massive heart attack on his bathroom floor before the ambulance could get there. You never knew how long you had.

Rick knew he had to convince Eve to grab their second chance at happiness while they could.

The only thing he knew to do was be with her as much as possible. That would be no hardship for him. She had a creative flair that had always impressed him. They had similar taste in movies and loved the same kind of music – no small thing he'd discovered when he'd dated some younger women. He loved Eve's strength and intelligence, her sense of humor and her willingness to be adventurous in bed.

He couldn't imagine a better woman for him than Eve. If only she would admit she wanted a man in her life. And that he was that man.

Chapter Twelve

A week later, Eve closed the shop and walked upstairs to her new home. She crossed the kitchen, poured a glass of wine and sat at her new table in front of her new window and let out a deep sigh of relaxation. She loved this place. Loved that it was all hers. Loved that she could do anything she wanted. Eat whatever she felt like. Curl up on her comfy new sofa and watch whatever she wanted on the TV.

But who had time to watch TV? Amy's wedding was only two weeks away. Eve was almost done weeding through what was left in the house. The new owners would take possession a week after the wedding.

And still she'd been spending way too much of her time with Rick. Or not anywhere near enough.

There was that wishy-washy side of her again. The optimistic side could see her spending the rest of her life with Rick. They enjoyed many of the same things, laughed at the same jokes, and burned up the sheets together. He'd helped her move her stuff into the apartment and she simply liked him. A lot.

The realistic side of her knew that if she wanted to

hold onto that independence she craved, she couldn't let a man get too important.

Even if she feared she was falling in love with him. Especially if she feared she was falling in love with him.

He snuck into her mind all times of the day or night. Every time she heard the siren wail from the fire hall down the street, she thought of Rick. Was there a fire? Was he driving the ambulance?

Every time she entered her apartment she remembered enjoying a romantic picnic in front of the window, dancing on the hardwood floor, and christening the bedroom with a wild bout of sex on Sunday afternoon.

Her phone rang and she knew without looking that it would be Rick. They'd taken to talking after work every day, even if they didn't see each other.

"Hey," he said when she answered. "How was your day?"

Even as she warmed to his soft voice and the knowledge that he cared about her and truly wanted to know how her day had gone, Eve wondered if things weren't getting a little too intimate. This was getting to be a little too...homey. A little too real. They'd agreed to play girlfriend and boyfriend—even though Rick hated the term—when they were out in public. Somehow, they'd started to get too close when it was just the two of them.

"Okay. How about yours?" she asked because she didn't want to be rude and she didn't know how to push him away without hurting him.

"Productive. Back on the Baxter kitchen remodel now."

"Good." What did she say now? How did she tell him they needed to take a step back? That she was feeling too much. Too fast.

When she didn't say anything else, he cleared his

throat. "Is everything all right?"

"Sure. Fine." And then she winced. He'd given her the perfect opening and still she couldn't say the words.

"I'm in the mood for tacos," he said, his voice still cheery. "What do you think? I can pick some up and bring them right over."

"It's Tuesday. Your dinner and drill night." He had to stop skipping important things for her. She didn't want to be the reason he neglected his duties with the department.

"They won't even miss me. But I miss you." His voice was soft and seductive.

"I can't tonight," she said quickly before she changed her mind. "You go to your drill. You should."

"It's driver's training tonight. I've been driving all of the rigs for a million years. I don't need it."

"I heard you never used to miss drills. You can't suddenly be changing your life for me."

"It's just been a couple of weeks. Come on, I'm hungry. I can be over to your place with food in less than thirty."

She was hungry and she missed him, but she couldn't weaken. Her mother had been weak. *She'd* been weak with Donald. "I've got plans for tonight, Rick. I can't."

"Oh. Okay." The disappointment in his voice was clear. Yeah, they'd gotten way too close. "How's that steam shower working for you? No problems?"

"No, it's great. I love it."

"Sure you don't want me to come over and check it out for you? *With* you?"

She laughed. She had to. Rick made her laugh and that was one of the things that was so great about him. "No. Now go. Meet the guys and do your thing at the fire hall. I'll see you later."

"Later tonight?" She could almost see the gleam in

his eyes, the hopeful expression on his face.

She had to stay strong. Still, she laughed. "No. You're impossible. Not tonight."

"But tomorrow's Wednesday."

"Very good. You know your days of the week."

"But you have your girls' night on Wednesday."

"Yeah?"

He huffed. "Nothing. I was thinking it was just too bad our nights out aren't on the same day of the week."

Well, maybe she could ask Maggie and Tess if they could change to Tues—wait. What the hell was she thinking? There she went, changing her life for a man. Again! No, no, no! "I have to go now. Bye, Rick."

Eve dropped her phone to the table and leapt from her chair. She would *not* change her life for a man again. She'd changed colleges to follow the boyfriend before Donald. She'd had a great job offer right out of college, but Don hadn't wanted to move across the country so she'd stayed in Best Bay. She'd never cooked with mushrooms because Don didn't like them and she never complained when he always wanted to be on top.

At least, she'd put her foot down about opening her business. Donald had been sure she'd lose her investment when she bought this building with money she'd inherited when her dad died, and then opened her small shop after Seth started school. The rent from the apartment had covered the building expenses and her shop held its own. And here she was finally, in the only place that had always been truly hers.

Tonight was all about relaxing. About doing what she wanted. Eating what she wanted for dinner. Making the time to watch what she wanted on her new TV, on her new sofa in her new living room. That was her plan for tonight.

She pulled out some cut veggies and a bowl of hummus and grabbed her glass of wine. Then she settled on her comfy sofa with a hum of satisfaction and chose a romantic comedy she'd always wanted to watch.

The plot was fast-paced and she laughed out loud at some of the banter between the two main characters. But when she turned to share the laugh, no one was there.

***

"What do you mean you don't have a dress yet?" Tess demanded as their dinners were served at O'Neill's. "What are you waiting for?"

"I don't know. I keep putting it off."

"So you want to go to your daughter's wedding in something you have hanging in your closet now?" Maggie asked.

"God, no."

"Then what are you waiting for?" Maggie repeated Tess's question.

Tess glanced at her watch. "If we leave now, we'll have a couple of hours shopping time in Erie."

"Great idea," Maggie said. "I'm game."

"But our food." Erie? They wanted to drive almost an hour at six o'clock in the evening so she could try on dresses she would hate?

Tess waved to their waiter. "Box these up, please."

Before Eve knew it, they'd stored the food in Eve's refrigerator, piled into Tess's SUV and headed down I-86. Her friends were right. She had to find a dress. And now she had to find a dress that fit perfectly because she wasn't going to have time to have it altered.

"Long or short?" Maggie asked as they walked into Tess's favorite dress shop. When Eve just stared at her, she added, "The dress. Long or short skirt?"

"Doesn't matter. But Amy was clear that it couldn't be hot or sexy. Or rather, I couldn't look hot or sexy in it."

"That's ridiculous," Tess snapped.

"Mothers of the bride are not allowed to look good. We're supposed to look old and frumpy. It's tradition."

"No, it's not," Maggie replied. "I guarantee I didn't look old or frumpy when Danielle got married."

"You were only thirty-nine at the time."

"I can't believe it was ten years ago. But anyway, I promise you could never look frumpy in anything."

"I refuse to let you buy something you look bad in," Tess chimed in. "You'll just have to keep trying them on until you find the right one."

Eve was exhausted just thinking about it. And now the racks of dresses seemed overwhelming. Maybe she could pull out that dress she'd worn to Heather's wedding. "I don't think I'm up to it."

"Why not?" Maggie asked. "What's going on?"

"Too much. The house. The apartment. The wedding."

"The boyfriend," Tess added. She grabbed some dresses in colors and styles Eve would have never chosen.

She let Tess tug her to the dressing rooms. "He's not really—"

"Oh, come on. Who are you trying to convince, because it's not me or Maggie." Tess shoved Eve into a free dressing room and handed her the dresses. "We see the way you and Rick are when you're together. We hear the way you talk about him. If you're not all the way in love with him, you're damn close."

Eve swallowed. "I know. I'm scared to death." She stared at her reflection in the mirror for a moment. The lights sent unflattering shadows over her, and she turned her back on the mirror as she undressed.

"What are you scared of?" Maggie asked.

"Losing my independence. Changing my life for a man again." She let out a deep sigh and pulled a little black dress over her head. "Losing myself."

"If it's the right man, you can find yourself," Tess said, almost as if to herself.

Eve turned back to the mirror. She'd thought it would be too short. Too tight. But it fit just right and looked...amazing. Even under the unflattering lights. She smiled to herself as she imagined Rick's expression when he saw her in it. "I don't think the mother of the bride is supposed to wear an LBD to the wedding."

"Let me see," Maggie called out.

"It's for the rehearsal dinner," Tess said. "Get out here."

"I forgot about the rehearsal dinner." Two dresses. Shit. She had to buy two dresses.

Maggie squealed when Eve stepped out. "I love it."

Tess just nodded with that know-it-all look on her face. "Rick will trip over his tongue when he sees you in that dress."

"It's not too sexy?" She didn't want Amy unhappy. It was her wedding after all.

"Just sexy enough. Look, barely any cleavage, just skims the knees. Your daughter can't possibly complain."

"And Rick will definitely love it," Maggie added.

Shouldn't she be buying the dress for herself? So she could feel good about herself? Women shouldn't dress just to please men. But she loved this dress. It was just an added benefit that it would make Rick's eyes spark too.

"Okay. One down. One to go."

***

Eve was confusing him. Rick knew other men who said they'd never figured women out, but up until now, Rick thought the whole man/woman thing was pretty straight-forward. At least with Cathy it had been simple and straight-forward.

They'd liked each other from the first day they met.

Their feelings for each other grew quickly and they spent all their time together. They were engaged before the first semester ended. Married as soon as they graduated. No question. No wavering.

But it was different with Eve. Maybe because they'd known each other for years before things changed. Maybe it was because their relationship started out with a lie. Maybe she didn't believe they could really care for each other because it started out as pretend. Why couldn't she believe their feelings were real now?

The rehearsal dinner was in full swing. Rick had known Blake's parents, Marie and George Foster for years. BBBuilders had renovated their kitchen a few years ago. They put on a good party at the local golf club where George was a member. The little speeches were over. The plates had been collected. Now it was down to drinks and conversation.

Eve had knocked him out when she opened her door to him in that form-fitting little black dress. The red lipstick made her smile even more alluring.

He hadn't been able to speak for a moment as his eyes made love to every curve. Her arms were bare, as were her legs below the knee-length hem. The heels of her black shoes were just high enough to be enticing. The neckline scooped to barely show her cleavage. All he wanted was to peel it off her and take her to bed.

But at the moment she stood across the banquet room with Amy and Blake, deep in discussion about something likely wedding-related. Rick wouldn't have even been here tonight if he hadn't been Eve's wedding date. They might have pretended to have a relationship, but the date was real. The date had never been a lie.

He stood at the bar, waiting for their drinks, people-watching. Don and Tiffany were talking with Marie and George. The young folks in the wedding party were laughing together at the other end of the bar.

Seth, who'd flown in from the west coast early that morning, hung on the fringes of the group but appeared exhausted.

The harried bartender finally delivered the drinks. Rick stopped by to speak to Seth before heading back to Eve. "Hey, bud," Rick said. He remembered when Seth was born. Watched him grow up to a fine young man. "How's it going?"

"Hi, Mr. Best. Everything's good. I'll be tired all weekend, but..."

"Hey, you're an adult now. It's okay to call me Rick."

Seth shrugged. "So you really like my mom?"

"Yeah. I do. She's easy to like."

The young man smiled. "Yeah, she is. Do you make her happy?"

"I hope so. She makes me happy, Seth. And I haven't been really happy for a while now." And that said it all, didn't it?

"I'm glad." Seth looked away and Rick followed his gaze to see that Don and Tiffany had joined the group at the end of the bar. Seth's eyes narrowed and he straightened. Set down his drink on the bar.

Rick didn't like the look of that. "How about you?" he asked Seth, more to distract him from whatever was in his head. He put his hand on the young man's shoulder. "How's life in California?"

Seth blinked and turned back to Rick. "Um...okay. I like my job. Lots of the good kinds of challenges every day. And I'm making some great friends. But it's good to get back home for a few days." His voice trailed off as he looked back to his father and his new wife. "Look at him. Thinks he's a kid again or something."

Before Rick could respond, Don looked over and saw Seth glaring at him. He broke off from the group and approached them.

"Hey, son."

Seth just frowned.

Don glanced to Rick and then back to Seth. "I get the feeling you've been avoiding me. I haven't seen you in months. Let's have a drink and talk."

Seth shook his head. "Don't want to talk to you." He glanced at Rick. "I'm going to say good-night to Mom and Amy and then head back to the house. I'm exhausted. See you later, Rick."

He couldn't miss the look of longing on Donald's face as his son walked away. Don's jaw tightened. He nodded to Rick and then walked away to join his wife.

Rick grabbed their drinks. By the time he got to Eve, Seth had left, and Amy and Blake were talking to someone else. Eve smiled her thanks to him as he handed her the glass, then her worried look slipped over her face.

"What happened over there? Between Seth and Don?"

"Nothing really. Don wanted to talk and Seth didn't. That was about it."

She sighed. "I think Seth's still angry at Don for breaking up our family, but Don *is* Seth's father. I hope they can work it out."

"How are you doing?" Rick asked.

"I can't believe I cried when Amy walked down the aisle during the rehearsal. What am I going to do tomorrow?"

He slid his arm around her waist. "I'll pack a lot of tissues in my jacket pockets."

She tipped her head and rested it on his shoulder. "Thanks. I think I'll need it." She sighed again.

"Getting tired?"

"Yeah."

"Did I tell you how sexy you are in that dress?"

"You might have." She looked up at him and smiled.

"I guess it makes the time I spent trying on dresses worth it."

She'd tried on dresses with him in mind? Rick liked the thought of that. "Definitely worth it."

"I didn't set out to buy a sexy dress. My daughter forbid it."

"It's not the dress that's sexy. It's you in it." His gaze heated her. "Did I tell you how much I'm looking forward to taking it off you?"

He barely whispered, but she glanced around as if someone might have heard him. Then she smiled again. "Not in so many words."

"I can say the words again, if you want."

"Not necessary." She stepped away, then leaned in so her lips brushed his ear. "Your place or mine?"

He chuckled. "Yours."

It was too late and they were too tired for much foreplay by the time they got back to Eve's apartment. The entire evening had felt like foreplay anyway to Rick, with Eve looking so sexy in that dress and throwing him those heated glances over to him even while surrounded by dozens of people.

So after he finally peeled that incredible dress off her even more incredible body, he lifted her into his arms and gently placed her on the bed. Then he shed his clothes, grabbed a condom and joined her there. When they were finally in each other's arms on her new pillow-top mattress, the kisses they shared were long, and slow, and very, very wet.

Eve slowly rocked beneath him, silently begging him for more. All the while her fingers tugged on his hair, and they took the kisses even deeper. Her soft moans filled the room. Her passion drove him on and he slid his hand between them to find her hot and wet between her legs.

"Eve," he murmured. "So soft."

"Yes," she whispered. "Touch me."

Rick toyed with her clit and her throaty gasp let him know when he'd reached the right angle, the right pressure. It wasn't long before she broke, coming apart in his arms. He held her as she writhed, as she smiled and gasped. When she caught her breath she cried, "Fill me, Rick. Take me."

She chanted his name like a prayer.

He was hard and ready, and slid into her in one long, slow push. Eve cried out and his moan echoed hers a moment later. This was it. This was perfect. She was perfect.

He loved her. He might have been falling for her before, but now he knew he'd completed the plunge. Eve had his heart. He loved her in a way he never thought he could. Never thought he would.

Rick wrapped his arms around her and held her close, her body moving with him in a sensual undulation. The dance of their bodies drove him on. Drove the love and the arousal and the need he had for her. When his orgasm hit, he emptied himself into her, his seed into her body, his love into her heart.

He caught her gaze and he could see the love in her eyes, even if she never admitted it in so many words. Tears glittered on her lashes. He hoped like hell they were because she was happy, and not because she was going to say good-bye.

Chapter Thirteen

The bride was beautiful, but Rick thought the mother of the bride outshone her daughter by a mile. Eve's eyes were bright even as her tears flowed during most of the ceremony. The neckline of her silky dress draped in some fancy way that called attention to her breasts while still keeping them fully covered. The hemline skimmed her knees and her light hair glowed against the deep red fabric, the color of the merlot Cathy used to drink.

The banquet hall was full of family and friends. Rick knew most of them. Eve had gone to check on the food and Rick headed straight for the bar. There was an edgy twist in his stomach and he couldn't figure out why it was there.

It probably was because his agreement with Eve ended tonight. He'd been her wedding date and after tonight the deal was off. He didn't want it to end. They'd made love with such emotion last night, but he knew she was going to want to break up when the reception was over. Or was she? Could she have looked at him with such longing, murmured his name with such need, if she didn't love him?

She did love him. He knew she did.

She hadn't returned to their table when he got back with the drinks like she said she would. He searched the hundreds of people in the room and didn't see the merlot-colored dress or the light blonde hair. She was still in the kitchen, he told himself. She was mingling with guests outside. She was checking on the whereabouts of the wedding party, who were still out having photos taken around the lake before coming here for dinner and dancing.

His heart began to hammer. Those were the kinds of things he'd told himself at Heather's reception when he couldn't find Cathy. He couldn't stop the memories from flooding in. The annoyance when Cathy had dashed away to drive home and pick up the missing gifts. The sudden panic when he realized how long she'd been gone. The frantic search to find her among the guests. He'd left his phone home because Cathy said it stuck out of his pocket like a sore thumb.

His friend, Ford Harper, chief of the Best Bay police department at the time, had found Rick in the crowd. Took him to a quiet corner to tell him about the accident. Rick's heart raced now as if it was happening all over again. He caught a glimpse of Ford, laughing with someone on Blake's side of the family. He'd retired from the force, though, so he might not have the inside connections anymore.

Rick peeked in the kitchen. Eve wasn't among the staff bustling to get the dinner ready. He stepped outside. Young kids were running and laughing, parents trying to keep them corralled and save their dressy clothes from getting grass-stained. He didn't see Eve with them or any of the other small groups killing time until the wedding party arrived.

He turned back inside. His mind wouldn't shut

down. Eve had ridden with him, so she didn't have a car here. Didn't have his keys. He supposed she could have borrowed someone else's car if she had to go somewhere, but why? She would have known he'd take her anywhere she wanted to go.

Would she have left without telling him? Yeah, she probably would. She was *independent*. Did she think she didn't have to take into consideration the people who cared about her?

Who would know where she'd gone? He spied Seth across the room and headed toward him. Surely he'd know. He was talking up a pretty girl with long brown hair, one of Clint Harris's daughters. What was her name? Zoey, maybe. Rick wanted to grab Seth and demand to know where Eve was, but he sauntered up and placed his hand on the young man's shoulder and kept his voice smooth and light.

"Hey, Seth. Have you seen your mom?"

Seth swept his gaze around the room. He shrugged. "She's around here somewhere. Did you text her?"

"Can't. She left her phone at home."

"Seriously?" The look of horror on his face, told Rick he couldn't imagine anyone not being chained to their cell phones. "Maybe she's outside waiting for the limo to get here. I've heard some of the guests are getting hungry."

"Maybe."

"Um, do you know Chloe Harris?" Seth asked. He smiled at the pretty girl beside him. "This is my mom's boyfriend, Rick Best."

"Hi." Rick cringed inwardly at *boyfriend,* but still managed a smile. "I know Chloe. Her dad's the fire chief."

"Oh sure. Well, I know Mom will show soon." Seth turned to leave with Chloe, then turned back to Rick. "Listen, I don't want to get all sappy but I just wanted to say I haven't seen my mom look this happy in a long time. I'm glad you're in her life. It makes me feel better, being all the way across the country, to know you're here for her." Seth threw his arms around Rick for a quick bear hug.

"Thanks, bud."

"You can hug him but you can't even talk to me?" Don came out of nowhere, his face a dark mixture of anger and hurt.

"I don't have anything to say to you," Seth said through gritted teeth.

"Seth..."

"You broke our family apart. You want to pretend you're some kind of kid again. But guess what, Dad. You're not. You just look stupid. Come on, Chloe." Seth grabbed her hand and stalked across the floor.

"What's going on?" Eve came up behind Rick and looked over his shoulder at Don.

The tension that Rick had been holding onto released with a huge rush of relief. He turned around and threw his arms around her. Tears stung his eyes, but he managed to blink them back and he hoped she never saw them. "Where have you been?" he murmured.

"In the bathroom with Maggie's granddaughter. The kids were running around and Suzy fell and skinned her knee. Maggie rounded up the boys while I applied a little first aid." She stepped away but smiled at him. "Why, did you miss me?"

"More than you know."

Tiffany was talking to Don in loud whispers. It appeared he wanted to follow Seth and she was holding him back. From what Rick had seen of their relationship, Tiffany seemed to be the more mature of the two.

"Here they come!" someone shouted. The bridal

party must have finally arrived.

***

A wedding reception was supposed to be a party. A good time, right? Eve wished she could say she was having a good time, but her stomach was so jumbled up with nerves she couldn't eat more than a couple of bites.

Sitting at the parents table with Don and Tiffany didn't help any. Don was in a bad mood after Seth walked away from him. Eve wished she could make things better between them, but she knew father and son were going to have to figure it out on their own.

Marie and George, her daughter's new in-laws were pleasant enough, but after the oh-wasn't-it-a-nice-wedding comments, there wasn't a whole lot of dinner conversation going on around the table. And once they were done with dinner, Rick seemed to want to hover. He'd never been that way before. She wondered if there had been more to the confrontation between Seth, Rick and Don, than what Rick had told her.

She had to get away from the table. She leaned over and kissed Rick's cheek. "I'm going to make the rounds. Come and find me when you want to dance."

He didn't try to stop her. "You got it."

Eve had managed to say hello to just about everyone when the DJ announced the father/daughter dance. *Already?* She turned to face the dance floor as Don took their daughter into his arms. She elbowed her way to the front of the crowd. She didn't want to miss this.

Amy looked like the little princess she used to dress up as when she was young. Tears sparkled in her eyes as she looked up at her father. Don had aged well. He was tall and handsome in his tuxedo. The love Eve saw in his eyes as he looked at their daughter reminded Eve of when she'd first fallen in love with him. There had been a lot of good times over the years and she couldn't forget that while she was dealing with the hurt and anger.

In fact, where was the hurt and anger? Eve took a deep breath and considered. They were still there, but they weren't the only emotions she felt. Maybe there was even some love left in her heart for the father of her children.

Amy and Seth were so different. Normally, Amy was the drama queen and Seth was the calm one. But Amy seemed to have taken the break-up of her parents' marriage much easier than Seth did. She'd had an emotional blow up at the time, but she seemed to get over it pretty quickly. Seth's emotions had just simmered and while Eve had thought he'd gotten over it too, obviously that wasn't the case.

Tiffany came up beside Eve. She wore a sky blue sheath that emphasized her tall, slender figure. She looked like a teenager, even though she was twenty-six. Eve braced for a confrontation, but Tiffany just threw her a smile. "Don't they look so great together?" she whispered. "Father and daughter on this special day. So happy."

Eve smiled back. "Yeah, they do. Amy was always Daddy's little girl."

"I'm sorry Seth is so upset," Tiffany said, ruining the moment. "I'm glad Amy's been more forgiving. It hurt Don a lot to have caused his children pain."

Eve tensed. What about the pain he'd caused her? But now wasn't the time to get into it, no matter how much she wanted to. The song wound down and the applause started as the dance finished. Eve walked away before she said something she'd regret.

Was Donald just as controlling with Tiffany as he'd been with Eve? Perhaps that was why he wanted a younger wife, although Eve had usually gone along with whatever Don had wanted for the entire length of their marriage. Why had she done that for so long? Had she been so weak she hadn't known what else to do? Or had she internalized her mother's don't-rock-the-boat philosophy?

She joined Tess standing alone over by the bar. She'd always envied her single friend for the independent life she led. Now Eve was free from Don and could make her own decisions. Pride at her new self-confidence made her smile. She reveled in her independence.

She had a home that she loved, the little apartment she'd made into her oasis. The first place of her own. Her forever home. She'd live there until she couldn't climb the stairs.

Eve turned to Tess. "Do you think I could put in an elevator up to the apartment?"

"Tired of climbing the stairs already?"

"No. Just thinking ahead."

"Not really my subject of expertise, but anything's possible. You should ask that handsome guy you've been hanging out with."

"Speaking of which, where's that cute kid you came with?" Eve didn't recognize him. Where did Tess find these guys?

Tess pointed to the dance floor. "He's with that group jumping around out there, pretending that's dancing. I'll claim him for a slow dance soon."

"Why does Don look foolish with a younger woman but you look sexy with a younger guy?"

"Don't you know I always look sexier than any guy?"

Eve laughed. "Maybe I *should* have taken you as my date." It would have avoided a lot of the tension she was feeling right now, but she would have hated to have missed her time with Rick.

***

Rick stood alone as the traditional wedding dances began. Father and daughter. Mother and son. His mind kept going back to Heather's wedding and as if she knew what he was thinking, his daughter came over and put her arm around his waist. She was Amy's matron of honor and wore a long dress in the same pink as the flowers on all the tables.

She rested her shoulder against Rick's. "It's still hard to smile at a wedding reception, isn't it? I can't help but think of Mom."

"Yeah, me too. I've been bugging Eve and I've realized I don't want to let her out of my sight because of what happened with your mom. I know Eve's not going anywhere. But I can't stop worrying. Can't stop this feeling that if I don't grab this second chance with her right this minute, it's going to slip through my fingers."

"Don't worry, Dad. You have time."

He and Cathy had thought they had all the time in the world. "No one knows that, sweetie. I don't want to waste any more time." Maybe Eve would agree for them to keep seeing each other after tonight. Would booty calls satisfy him? No, he was sure that wouldn't be enough.

"Then...I don't know...ask her to marry you. Let her know you're serious."

"Marriage?" The idea didn't freak him out like he thought it might. It felt...right. It felt...crazy. "I don't know if it's the right time for that."

"The right time, did you say?"

"I think it's too early for a proposal."

"Remember you told me that if you wait for the right time, you'll never do it?" She'd been talking about trying for a baby.

"I remember."

"Well, we didn't wait."

"What? Do you mean..."

His little girl beamed. "Yeah. I'm pregnant. You're going to be a grandpa."

Grandpa. That would take getting used to. He gathered her into his arms. "I'm so happy for you, sweetie."

"I'm happy too. Scared. Maybe even terrified. But mostly just really happy."

"Are you announcing it to the world yet?"

"Just you and Ryan's parents for the time being. But you can tell Mrs. C."

His little girl was going to be a mother. This seemed like even more of a jolt than when she got engaged. Of course, he'd been able to share that announcement with Cathy. He was alone with this one.

But then he realized he wasn't alone. He had a big family and so did Ryan. And he had Eve. This baby would have so many people to love.

He and Heather stood for a minute, watching the dancing as other couples were joining the bridal couple on the dance floor. "So what are you going to do? With Mrs. C.?"

"I'm going to ask her to dance. And then I'll see what happens next." He kissed Heather's cheek and crossed the floor.

She stood with Tess at the edge of the dance floor. Rick had noticed Eve's friend had brought a date, a young man with spiky blond hair he didn't recognize. Apparently, Tess never lacked for a date.

Eve watched him approach, a smile lighting up her face. He paused in his approach, just to soak in the sight of her. He'd never tire of seeing her, being with her. He was sure of that. He wanted to be with her for the rest of his life.

He said hi to Tess, then turned to Eve. "Would you like to dance?"

"I'd love to."

As he pulled her into his arms on the dance floor, he saw Ryan bring Heather out too. He was so glad Heather had Ryan to love her and take care of her. "I just got some exciting news," he whispered to Eve.

"What?"

"No one else knows." He kissed her ear. "Heather is expecting."

A short squeal escaped Eve's lips before she clamped one hand over her mouth. "That's wonderful."

"Yeah. The world keeps changing so fast it's hard to keep up."

The music shifted smoothly from one slow song to another, so he kept her out on the floor. If he had his way, they'd play only slow songs and he'd keep Eve in his arms for the rest of the night.

For the rest of his life.

"I've fallen in love with you," he murmured. He couldn't keep it to himself any longer. "I didn't plan on it but no matter what you think about it, I'm glad I have."

"Oh, Rick. I love you too." Her tone of voice didn't sound as happy as his did.

But that's what he'd been waiting to hear. "I'm glad. Now we don't have to break up at the end of the night."

She tripped over his feet and after he steadied her, she paused where they were in the middle of the dance floor. "No. It doesn't change anything."

People dancing around them sent them curious glances but Rick ignored them. "How can you say that? It changes everything. Love changes everything."

"But love isn't always enough."

"Are you saying you don't love me enough to stay with me?"

Eve grabbed his wrist. "We can't do this here." She tugged him off the floor and out the front door and into the muggy night air.

A few people were mingling outside. Rick saw Maggie minding her grandchildren as they ran around in the side lawn. A few couples were kissing in the shadows. He turned to Eve, but she pulled him further into the shadows.

She was shaking, trembling. He should have known she would freak out. Should have known this wasn't the time to pin her down, not the right time to shake things up and suddenly crave a commitment. But the panic had built up quickly and unexpectedly. It might not have been the right time, but he couldn't wait any longer. His heart pounded and he couldn't slow down his breathing.

"Rick, what's going on?"

He thought of Cathy, taken in a senseless car accident. He thought of Max's friend, taken by a sudden heart attack. As a first responder, too many times over the years he'd responded to a deadly accident or illness. All those people had thought they had all the time in the world too. He had to grab this chance with Eve.

This was the right time.

"Eve. I'm so glad we've had these weeks to get to know each other again. I'm so glad you love me like I love you. This is our second chance at happiness. We have to grab it now before it's too late."

Her expression softened. "Cathy. Of course, I'm sorry. I didn't think about how you might feel at the reception. I should have been more considerate."

"It's not that. Or it's not *just* that." He took her into his arms and she let him, so he was encouraged. "It's you. You and me. It's only been a few weeks but I'm happier when I'm with you. I can't imagine my life without you."

"Rick..."

He had to get the words out before that uncertain

look on her face made him hesitate. “I love you. Marry me, Eve. Stay with me. Let me take care of you. Marry me, Eve. Live with me and be my wife.” His pulse thudded in his ears. He held his breath as he watched her reaction, waited for a response. But her arms dropped from around his neck and as the color faded from her face, he realized sometimes it didn’t matter if it was the right time.

“Did you hear what you said?” Her voice was rough, her eyes accusing. “You may think you love me but I guess you don’t know me at all.”

The panic hit him again. What did he say? What did he say wrong? The panic burst into irritation which flared to anger. “I told you I loved you. That I wanted to marry you, spend my life with you. Shouldn’t that be enough?”

“Maybe it should be. But it’s not enough for me. It can’t be.” Sadness, not anger, colored her voice. “Your words were all wrong, Rick. You should have known that.”

“I refuse to weigh every word that comes out of my mouth,” he snapped, fear gnawing at his spine. “I’m a straight-talking man, you know that. I say what I mean and I don’t play games.”

“I’m not playing either, Rick. This is important to me.”

“And it’s not important to me?” A voice in the back of his head, the one from his heart, screamed at her to explain. To beg her to tell him what she wanted him to say. But he couldn’t spend the rest of his life like that. “I guess you don’t know me very well, either.”

She wouldn’t look at him, wouldn’t say anything more. How could she think he’d be satisfied with her answer?

“Do I have to demand an explanation? I think you owe me that much. What did I say then that was so terrible?"

"You want to take care of me."

"God, of course I know you can take care of yourself. But part of loving someone is wanting to take care of them. You can take care of me too. Is that better?"

"You want me to move in with you." Accusation was in her voice.

"Of course, I do. If we got married we'd be living together, that's for sure." But there was a little niggle in the back of his mind that told him there was something important he wasn't getting.

She took a step back. "I don't want to move in with you."

He flinched at the slow words, the dark tone. "I guess that answers my question, then, doesn't it?"

He couldn't stay there any longer, surrounded by the sounds of celebration, staring at the woman who refused to let him into her heart. Rick turned and walked away, knowing he'd lost his chance to spend the rest of his life with Eve, as surely as he had with Cathy.

Chapter Fourteen

Move in with him?

The music was blaring, the reception still going strong. Eve sank to a bench, her knees trembling.

Move in with him?

Didn't he understand? Didn't he know, after helping her for weeks to turn her apartment into her home, the first home that was all hers? He should know she wouldn't want to leave it behind and move in with him. How could he ask her to do that as if it was nothing?

Her pulse thudded in her ears like a death knell. Her chest was hollow. Her head whirling. She closed her eyes against the spotlights illuminating the building. What happened? How could this have happened?

"Mom?" Seth appeared, his hands clenched at his sides, but the anger on his face quickly turned to concern. "Are you okay?"

No. "I'm fine. What's the matter?"

"I almost had it out with Dad again, I had to get away."

"Oh, Seth."

He paced the ground in front of her. "I'm going to go home."

"You've been drinking. Do you want me to drive you to the house? Oh, wait. I can't." She'd come with Rick. And he'd left.

"No, that's okay. Chloe is going to drive me but I'm not staying in Best Bay." He sat down beside her. "I'm going to catch the first flight out."

"Wait. You were going to stay until Monday. We haven't had any time together."

"I...I don't know, Mom. I thought I was okay with what Dad did. Breaking up our family. Walking out on you. But I'm not. I'm really not." Seth started to rise.

Eve had to shut down the part of her brain that was crying out for Rick, wondering how everything had gone so wrong, so fast. Her son needed her now.

"Let's talk a minute." She took his hand to stop him from leaving. He couldn't leave this way. "What will you gain by leaving tonight? What's a couple of more days?"

"I don't want to deal with Dad. Watch him around...Tiffany," he sneered. "Did you know she was between Amy and me in school?"

"Of course, I know." Eve said it as softly as she could.

"How could he have done it? An affair with someone so much younger than him? Is that what's called a mid-life crisis?"

"Maybe. I have to be honest with you, Seth. For me, it doesn't matter how old the other woman is, your father didn't want to be married to me anymore. But that doesn't mean he doesn't still want to be your dad. He still loves you guys. Don't ever doubt that."

"Did you know why I took the job out west?"

"Because it was a great job?"

"Yeah, it was, but I was offered almost as good a job

around here. But I wanted to get away. I didn't want to go out with my friends and see my dad hanging out with a bunch of other people my age."

"Your dad did what he did. He must have been unhappy. I'm sure he didn't make the decision lightly." How did she find herself defending Don? "All you can do now is decide how you're going to deal with it. You can sneak back to San Diego and ignore your father. Let the gulf between you grow wider until there's no way to ever breech the gap, and you two could be estranged forever.

"Or you could be the adult that you are and make peace with him. You don't have to be happy with his choices, but see, when you come right down to it, the only thing you can control is your reaction. It's your choice how you handle things. Your choice what attitude you take with him."

A metaphorical light bulb went off above Eve's head. She'd been blaming Don for her lousy attitude. Blamed Don for turning into a person she didn't like when she was around him. But those were choices she made too. She wasn't going to let him order her around, but she could choose not to give him attitude back.

She chuckled sadly and put her arm around Seth's shoulders. "Your dad's just trying to make this new family dynamic work. To try to fit the pieces into a new picture of what our family is going to be now. It may not make you comfortable to see him with Tiffany, but she's his wife now. I think you should give your dad the benefit of the doubt." Even if Eve thought Don didn't really deserve these great kids.

"I get what you're saying, Mom. It's up to me how I act around Dad and Tiffany. It's my choice if I want to get angry and punch him out. It's my choice if I smile and curse him out silently behind his back. It's my choice if I avoid him for the rest of my life."

Eve stared at him, vaguely alarmed, and Seth smiled at her. “Maybe I’ll just avoid him for the rest of the night.” He gave her a sweet kiss on the cheek. “I’m going to head out with Chloe but I’ll stay here until Monday. Tomorrow I’ll sort through my junk and see what I want to keep.”

“Give Amy a kiss before you leave.”

“I will.”

Eve watched her baby, her grown son, saunter away. If she’d helped him deal with his anger and make peace with his father, she’d be happy.

But how long before Eve would really be happy again?

***

What the hell?

Rick roared down the street in his pick-up, wishing he was on the interstate and not on a stupid village street with a thirty mile per hour speed limit. How could he release any stress that way?

Eve didn’t want to be with him. She couldn’t have stated it more clearly than that. It was like a kick in the gut. One minute she said she loved him. The next minute she told him she didn’t want to live with him.

What. The. Hell.

How could he have gotten it so wrong? Were her words all lies, pretending she cared for him, like they’d been doing for the past few weeks? He’d stopped pretending weeks ago. He may never have been pretending.

Maybe Eve had always been faking it. Maybe she didn’t really love the feel of his skin under her fingertips. Maybe she didn’t really enjoy those long kisses. Maybe *I love you* were just words to her.

She was right. Maybe he’d never known her at all.

He could stop at the BB&G and get roaring drunk but Jimmy wouldn’t let him. And Jimmy would get the word out that Rick was drinking away his sorrows before he ever crawled home. He was trying to remember how much liquor he had at home. Less than a six-pack of beer. That would never be enough to wipe her out of his mind. He had a bottle of some kind of bourbon that John liked but Rick had no idea how much was in the bottle. There were a few bottles of wine in the rack. If he drank it all he'd be puking his brains out in the morning, but at least he'd have gotten his mind off Eve stomping on his heart.

He was almost home when the call came through. House fire, smoke and flames visible. Back across town, just a couple of blocks from the banquet facility he'd left behind. He turned his truck around, flipped on his blue light, and raced to the fire hall. Looked like he'd have something else to distract him tonight.

***

Now that the disaster with Seth was averted, the memory of the fiasco with Rick rushed back into her brain. They'd been planning to break up all along. Eve was sure most of the people inside heard enough of the beginning of their argument to believe it when she said it was over.

It was over.

She sniffed. She was not going to cry. But her eyes didn't listen and tears leaked out anyway. Eve closed her eyes and swiped at them with her fingers. No tears. She'd known this time was coming. She should have expected the pain in Rick's expression. Should have known how sharp it would be in her chest.

Someone sat down beside Eve. The sharp spicy scent told her it was Tess. Eve opened her eyes and Tess put her arm around Eve.

"Something happen with Seth?" Tess asked.

"He's pretty mad at his dad, but I think we got it straightened out."

"That's not what's making you cry then."

"I'm not crying."

"Don't lie to me. What happened?"

"Rick asked me to marry him."

Tess lifted a brow. "From the way you look it must have been the worst proposal in the history of men getting down on their knees."

"He wants me to move in with him."

"Married people usually live together," Tess replied dryly.

"But he just finished remodeling my new place. He knew how important it was to me. At least I thought he did. Why would he think I'd be okay with moving out of it? I don't want to move out of it."

"Sweetie, you didn't turn down his proposal because you had to choose between a tiny apartment and a big house. Tell me you didn't."

"Not entirely." As she thought about it, she knew that wasn't really the problem. At least not the biggest part. "I thought he knew me. But he didn't even offer to move in with me. It never would have occurred to him, would it?"

Tess shrugged. "He has a bigger place."

"You're no help if you're going to side with him."

"Hon, I'm always on your side. But I think we have to talk about the bigger problem."

"Yeah? What's that?"

"What is the pull that apartment has on you?"

"It's mine! One thing that's mine."

"You have lots of things. Lots of people. Your kids. Your friends." Tess shifted on the bench to nail her with her gaze. "You even have your own successful business. Would marrying Rick take that away from you?"

"No. But my business has never been a part of this. Never a part of the problem."

"What's the problem?"

"I want my independence. I don't want to ever change my life for a man again." She didn't want to be a doormat. "I want to make my own choices. I want my own place. I love that place. I just got it. And he knew how important it was to me and he didn't care."

"Of course he cares. He just loves you enough to think you'd want to be with him all the time."

And when Tess said it that way, Eve knew she was right. "I know. And I do love him too."

"So again, what's the problem?"

"I'm afraid I'll end up weak again. Changing my life for a man. Not able to make my own choices."

"Let's stop right there."

The sharp tone of Tess's voice made Eve freeze. "What?"

"I've heard you talk all kinds of shit about how you didn't take that job with the start-up company down south right out of college because Don didn't want to move. Did he twist your arm? Did he chain you to the kitchen stove? Did he threaten to kill your firstborn child?"

"Don't be ridiculous."

"So it was your decision. Your choice."

"We were married."

"So Don could have gone with you if he really loved you. Or you could have gone without him and maybe one of you would have sent the other divorce papers out of the blue instead of following to get the other back." Tess cleared her throat after that outburst but before Eve could process her words, her friend grasped her hands. "But the truth is that it was your choice to stay here."

She was right. "Yeah." But did Eve make those choices for herself, or for the man in her life? "It's cut and dried for you, isn't it?"

"Don't second guess yourself, sweetie. What's done

is done. You have a great guy who loves you now and you have a choice to make. Don't let him get away because you think you don't have a choice. You always have a choice."

Tess was right. She was always right. Eve had been so afraid to try with Rick that she'd made a knee-jerk decision and then blamed him for it. There had to be a way to work it out. It didn't have to be either/or. She didn't have to marry him or lose him forever. There had to be a way to compromise.

But that was never going to happen if they didn't talk. "I have to call him." She reached for her phone but of course, the dress she was wearing had no pockets, and she'd left her phone at home anyway. "Do you have your phone?"

"It's inside. Come on."

As they rose from the bench, they heard the first sirens. "Oh no." Eve looked around, saw the smoke rising close by. She could smell the smoke now. Were those flames? "Oh no."

She ran down the sidewalk as fast as she could in her heels, in the direction of the smoke. Tess was right behind her, cursing a blue streak. Some of the other wedding guests followed, talking excitedly.

Rick would be on the scene, she was certain of it. He'd be fighting this fire, just as he went to all the other emergency calls, volunteering to put his life on the line for others who needed him.

She could see the lights flashing before they hit the end of the block. Tess caught up with her at the corner and took her arm. "Hon, we're going to be in the way."

"I just have to see him."

Tess tugged at her. "You won't be able to see him. Look at all the coats. Hats. Boots. You're not going to be able to pick him out unless you get close and you can't get that close. You know you can't."

Half a block away, Eve could hear the crackling of the fire. Could feel the heat from the flames. She'd never been this close to a building on fire before. "How can they go in there?" she whispered.

Eve wished she could forget about her friend, Bonnie, who'd lost her firefighter husband. Wished she didn't think about Rick going into that inferno. What if something happened to him tonight? What if he died, thinking she didn't love him enough to work things out? What if he never knew she'd been on her way to tell him?

He was right. They could never assume they had all the time in the world. She hoped she wasn't too late to grab that chance with Rick.

More trucks were rushing to the scene, some from neighboring departments and she knew Tess was right. They would be in the way. A crowd of gawkers had begun to gather on the corner and Eve didn't want to be a part of that.

"Let's go back. I want to see Amy and Blake before they leave on their honeymoon." And by then maybe she'd know what to say to Rick.

***

Rick and the rest of the department had been at the fire scene for most of the night. It had been one of those big old houses that had been divided into two apartments. They were able to save the structures around it from more than just some scorched siding, but the house was a total loss.

He was stumbling from exhaustion. Soaking wet from sweating inside the heavy turn-out gear. Filthy from the soot and grime of a fire scene. A couple of guys from the county fire investigation team were picking through the ruins, though it was obvious the guy in the lower apartment had fallen asleep with a cigarette. He was lucky to have made it out of the burning building in his underwear.

A young woman, barely out of her teens, dark hair pulled back in a straggly ponytail, was pacing the sidewalk. She wore a white tank top and pink flannel pants with...were those penguins on them? Rick wondered if she'd been there all night. Paul Edwards, the department chaplain, must have been called down to help her. As Rick drank a bottle of water, he overheard the young woman talking to Paul.

"It was my first apartment. My place. My things. I lost everything. What am I going to do now?" Her mascara had dried in dark streaks down her cheeks.

"Do you have family or a friend we can call?" Paul asked.

"I...I left home on bad terms with my family. I fought with my mom. Bad. I wanted to do it all on my own. But I don't know what to do now."

"I can help you," Paul told her. "Why don't you let me call your mom?" Their words faded as he led her away.

Rick had stopped over to the rehab area that had been set up near the ambulance. All night EMTs checked blood pressures, made sure they didn't get overheated, pushed bottles of water at them, and basically gave them a chance to rest before they went back into battle.

Joe was there too. He grasped a bottle of water but he wasn't drinking it, he was staring at the smoking shell of a house across the street. Rick walked over to him.

"Bad memories?" Rick asked. Sometimes guys wanted to talk and sometimes they didn't, but it helped to know someone was willing to listen.

Joe blinked and shrugged. "They never really go away. No matter how many fires I've fought since then, I still see Frank buried under those beams."

It was never easy losing a fellow firefighter, but losing a good friend was even worse. And the survivors had to run into more burning buildings, never knowing if it would be their last. Couldn't think about the possibility.

Rick clapped Joe on the back. "Let's get this cleaned up so we can go home and get some rest. If we're lucky, we'll have a few hours with no falls or chest pains or burnt popcorn."

Joe nodded.

The battle was over now. All that was left was the clean-up. And the recovery. Rick downed another bottle of water and looked forward to a shower and collapsing into bed. But first they had to finish rolling the hose and loading the trucks so they'd be ready for the next fire.

He hadn't had a chance to think about Eve, at least not much. He'd pushed it to the back of his mind because he didn't want to be distracted by his grief. Didn't want to obsess about his words. And hers. Not yet. He had to get some sleep first. At the moment all he could see was the shock and disappointment on her face.

And he knew that somehow, she thought he'd let her down.

Rick showered off the soot and grime and then fell into bed as the sun was rising. He shouldn't have been surprised by the dream. Eve was the one wandering on the sidewalk in front of the burning building. Of course, in the dream it was her building. The one with the brick façade. With the shop on the first floor and her apartment on the second. Over and over she chanted the words the young girl had cried to Paul.

My first apartment. My place. My things.

In the dream he let the building burn and his words to Eve echoed through his brain.

Live with me. Live with me. Live with me.

Rick shot up in bed. Sunshine lit the room. He rubbed his blurry eyes. His body ached from the punishment he'd put it through last night. But his head ached worse as he regretted the words he'd used in his spontaneous proposal.

Live with me.

Not an unusual thing to expect from the woman you wanted to spend the rest of your life with. Unless that woman had just moved into her first apartment. Had renovated it and furnished it with all her things.

How could he have forgotten her pride at renovating and moving into the first place she'd ever been able to call her own? How could he have tossed out words that in effect told her to forget about all that and just move in with him, when that wasn't what he meant at all.

She'd told him so many times that she was afraid she'd fall back into the same life she had before and she didn't want that life any more. And what had he done but offer her that life all over again? That same life she didn't want.

If he wanted to entice Eve into spending the rest of her life with him, he was going to have to offer her something different. A new picture into which they could fit all the pieces of their lives.

He glanced at the clock. It was after noon already. He had some shopping to do. This time he was going to do it right.

***

Eve wandered her apartment. She loved this place but her footsteps echoed as she paced the floor. It had been only one day, but she missed Rick. If they couldn't work things out, she knew she'd miss laughing at movies together. Talking about family and friends and what was going on in Best Bay. And okay, she would seriously miss the sex. And the kissing.

He was such a fabulous kisser. His kisses were so much more than lips. The whole body became involved. The emotions were involved.

She'd talked to Heather and knew that he was okay. There had been no fatalities but the house was a total loss. She'd left him a message on his phone, but since he'd been up all night, she knew he'd be sleeping. Eve didn't know what to do with her day. She'd been looking forward to a lazy day after the crazy busy last couple of days, but now all she wanted to do was talk to Rick.

It had been a lovely wedding, aside from the marriage proposal disaster. Amy and Blake were off on their honeymoon for a week in New York City.

Eve had decided to follow her own advice and choose her attitude with her ex-husband. She was happy she was no longer married to Don, so why should she care if he was married to Tiffany? *He* was the cliché, a middle-aged man marrying a woman young enough to be his daughter. If Tiffany made him happy, she wouldn't begrudge him that. She'd talked with Donald when she got back to the reception, told him she didn't want them to be enemies. He backed down on his attitude too and she was hopeful for a better relationship with her ex.

She could go over to the house, but Seth and Chloe were there this afternoon, going through his stuff. They'd met her for breakfast and seemed to be very into each other. She wondered what was going to happen with them. They'd been casual friends in high school, but meeting again at the reception might have caused a spark. But would a long distance relationship work for them?

How did it work for anyone?

But that wasn't the problem with her and Rick. They were in the same town, but other things besides physical distance could keep people apart. Would they be able to compromise? Oh God, she hoped they'd be able to compromise.

She'd texted Rick too and said she wanted to talk, but so far had gotten no reply. Was he still sleeping? It was almost dinner time. Was he going to ignore her? Of course, he was angry. He'd put his heart on the line and she'd shot him down. She'd just been so shocked. She hadn't expected a marriage proposal after only two months. Not after saying they were going to break up.

But hadn't she known they were too far gone to pretend they'd only been playing at a relationship? Hadn't she known she didn't want to live without him? Why had she been so afraid?

Her phone rang. She grabbed it and then tried not to be disappointed to see it was Maggie.

"Come down to the BB&G," Maggie said. She'd called to check on her earlier in the day. Tess had told Maggie what had happened with Eve and Rick the night before.

"I'm not hungry."

"I know you. You're pacing and worrying and thinking too much. Tess is meeting us there. You need something to take your mind off you know who."

Eve didn't want to keep pacing her empty apartment. Maggie was right, she was thinking too much. Second guessing everything about her and Rick. Some laughs with her friends was just what she needed. She threw on a pair of shorts and a tank top, slid her feet into some sandals and was out the door.

She loved how close she was to everything now. Her shop was a staircase away. The beach was a couple of blocks. The Best Bar and Grill was only a block away in the other direction.

She saw Maggie in the dining room as soon as she stepped in. As she walked past the bar area, she caught familiar voices. The Best brothers. She hesitated, then continued to Maggie's table, forcing herself not to look at the bar. She took the seat across from Maggie, sitting with her back to the bar.

"The grandkids went back home?" Eve asked. Maggie's daughter was having marital problems and Maggie had been watching her grandchildren more than usual. It was why she'd had them at the reception last night and had to keep her eye on them instead of enjoying the party.

"Yes. I miss them when they're gone, but whew, they wear me out."

"Hey, Eve!" A shout came from the bar. It sounded like Rick's brother, John. "Your boyfriend's over here!"

"Shut up." That loud whisper was Max.

"You mean, he's over there?" Eve whispered. How dare he be drinking with his brothers while she agonized alone in her apartment?

"Of course." Maggie smiled. "Why do you think I called you?"

Anger flared. "He could hang out at the bar but ignored my messages?" She refused to look around at him because then she had to wonder if he was still mad at her.

Maybe he didn't want to talk with her ever again, her realistic side said to her. Then that darn optimistic side said that maybe he was dying to talk to her but was waiting for her to make the first move, since she was the one who refused him. Since she was the one who had gone on and on about wanting to make her own choices.

Only one way to find out. "Be right back," she said to Maggie. Then she stood and whipped around. And then there was Rick, standing there with what her father would have called a shit-eating grin. She froze.

"Hello, Eve," he said, keeping an arm's length away from her.

"You can do better than that!" Max called out. "Tell

her you were wrong."

"Beg her forgiveness!" John shouted.

Rick tipped his head in the direction of the bar. "Family."

"Gotta love them," Eve replied, her voice a little rusty.

Rick opened his arms to her. "Come here, sweetheart."

Tears sprung to her eyes as she stepped into his embrace. It was like coming home. Applause rang out around them.

She didn't want him begging for anything. She was in the wrong. "We need to talk," she told him.

He nodded. "Yeah, we do. You want to take this outside?"

"Good idea."

He glanced to Maggie. "I'll bring her back in a few minutes."

"Don't take too long," her friend replied.

"You can keep her," Tess said, coming up behind them. "Take as long as you want."

"No," Maggie whispered loudly, her eyes wide. "I want to hear what happens."

"Go," Tess said, shooing them away.

Rick took Eve's hand and led her through the back door of the restaurant, into the alley that ran behind the buildings. He walked silently with her, fingers threaded together, down the block until they were standing behind her building. "We had our first kiss right here. Do you remember?"

"Of course, I remember."

He pointed up to the wonderful window he'd installed for her. "I thought about waiting under your big window with a bunch of flowers in my hand, but I didn't know how long it might take for you to notice me. Especially if you were watching one of those romantic comedies you love so much."

She would have loved to have seen him standing there, flowers in hand. Flowers. Candles. Picnic in an empty room. Rick had turned out to be quite the romantic. "I couldn't sit still to watch a movie today."

Rick led her across the alley to the community garden Cathy had helped to start. He'd installed a bench in the center in her memory. He drew Eve down beside him. "Why not, sweetheart?"

"I was thinking about you, of course. Thinking how stupid I was to push you away, to refuse you without even talking about it." She could make excuses, how she was overwhelmed with the wedding and Donald and Seth and her feelings for Rick. But the truth was, she was still scared she'd fall back into that old life. "I was scared even though I know you're nothing like my father."

"Your father? You don't talk much about your father."

"Well, you're nothing like him. He was a dictator."

Rick's face darkened. "Mean? Abusive?"

"No, not abusive," she hurried to say. "I mean, he never hit us or anything like that. Never. But he didn't like to be challenged. What he said, was the way it was. And my mom was a doormat. And I guess I was too."

"You were a kid."

"Yeah, but I guess I learned early not to rock the boat. Probably why I didn't see anything wrong with Don patting my head and telling me he'd take care of all the decisions. Still controlling, just in a different way." She grabbed his hand. "But I know you're not like them. I know it."

Rick cupped her face and dropped a soft kiss on her lips. "Thanks for telling me about your parents. Now I can see even more how wrong I was."

"No, *I* was wrong."

"Are we going to keep tossing the argument back and forth?"

She smiled through her tears. "Probably. I was wrong because I forgot that I always have a choice. Even whether or not to rock the boat."

"And I was wrong." He placed a finger over her lips to stop her from going on. "You were right. I said the wrong words to you the first time around. I'd like to try again if you'll let me."

Her stomach fluttered. Or was it her heart? "Okay."

"I love you, Eve. I love your warmth and your strength and your independence. I love laughing at funny movies with you and I love the way you kiss."

"I love the way you kiss too."

He dropped a quick, hard kiss on her mouth. "I know you're not interested in a traditional marriage, but I need to make a promise to you. A commitment. So these are my words to you." He took her hands and the intensity of his gaze made it hard for her to breathe. "Eve Corcoran. Will you be engaged to me for the rest of your life?"

She let out a teary laugh.

"This is my promise to you," he went on. "If you choose me, I will be yours. You will be mine. And I don't care if we ever get married. No, that's wrong. I would love it if we got married, but we don't have to. We'll have made the commitment to each other. You keep your apartment. I'll keep my house." He kissed her again. "And you can rock the boat whenever you want. I'll weather the storm with you."

He pulled a small jewelry box out of his pocket. "Eve, I beg you to never call me your boyfriend again. But you can call me your fiancé for the rest of your life."

Her heart was overflowing. Her mind was overwhelmed. But she had no question what she was going to say. "Yes. Yes, Rick. You do know me. You knew the perfect words to say."

Rick opened the ring box and lifted the ring from the velvet. She gave a little gasp. "I know it's not a traditional style engagement ring," he said, "but hey, we'll start our own traditions now, right?"

The stone was a large round diamond, that was traditional enough, but it was set into a series of interwoven strands of silver that created the wide band. To Eve it represented not only their promise to each other, but the way all the pieces of their lives would fit into the new life they would create together.

"It's lovely." She held out her hand and he placed it on her finger. It fit perfectly and she knew she'd made the right decision. She could have chosen the independent life she thought she wanted. And been lonely. Or she could embrace a life with a man who wouldn't ignore her or look down on her, but would support her and laugh with her and help make this new life an amazing journey.

Eve placed her hand on his cheek, the diamond sparkling in the fading sunlight. "I'm so glad I chose you."

Read on for sneak peeks at upcoming Silver Fox Romance releases!

RESCUE ME – Silver Fox Romance book #2 – Coming Soon

After years of playing it safe, Bonnie Petrowski's first attempt at being wild and spontaneous leaves her spinning off the road during a blinding snowstorm. The sassy widow has few regrets, but never owning up to her feelings for her late husband's best friend is one of them. And now it might be too late.

Firefighter Joe Waterman isn't going to let a little thing like a blizzard stop him from getting the hell away from his big empty house. He doesn't get far, however, before discovering a small car buried in the snow. When he recognizes his friend's widow inside, his unwanted attraction to her still blazes hot enough to melt the snow piling up around them. After he rescues her, not only do the sparks continue to zap between them - Bonnie wants to talk about their *feelings* for each other.

Joe made a promise years ago and he's bound to keep it. Even if it means he and Bonnie can never have a chance at forever together.

Excerpt:

"Joe? Thank God!" Relief whooshed through Bonnie's system. As did a crazy rush of awareness.

She'd finally gotten free of the freaking seat belt when she saw the headlights come up behind her. She'd scrambled for her purse, trying to ignore all the reminders whispering in the back of her head that creeps often preyed on stranded motorists. She didn't have anything she could use as a weapon in the car either.

But then she'd turned around and saw that it was Joe.

She let herself smile. Everything would be okay now. Bonnie leaned away from the bright flashlight. The car began to shift and she shrieked.

"Are you okay?" he called.

"Yeah. I'm fine. Can you help me out of here?"

He pulled on the door but the snow was obviously too high and heavy. His feet went out from under him. He cursed and hauled himself to his feet. Frantically, Bonnie pushed at the door, but it only opened a crack. Enough to let in the blowing wind and snow, but nowhere near enough to escape. She was trapped! Panic began to build as the snow swirled around her.

"Don't worry," he said calmly. "If I can't get the other door open, I'll get the shovel out of my truck."

He carried a shovel?

Joe pushed the door shut. "I'm going around to the other side now." At least, that's what she thought he said. The wind was loud, even with the door shut, and her blood was rushing through her ears. Joe Waterman. Who could have imagined he would be the one to come to her aid?

The windows were covered with snow, but she could see the flashlight and his shadowy figure circle her car, stumbling through the heavy snow. She'd hate it if he got hurt because of her.

Joe kept sinking in the snow, she could see him taking steps and stumbling, falling. She had to do something, not sit there like a bump and wait for him to save her.

Bonnie climbed over the console and used the hard surface to give her leverage. The car shifted more as she moved inside. She lifted the latch on the passenger door and pushed. Joe grabbed the handle and pulled it open.

And there he was, like an abominable snowman superhero.

"Hey," she said.

"Are you hurt?" He climbed into the passenger seat and pulled the door closed behind him. Snow fell off his hat and coat, settling inside the car along with what had already blown in. He checked her over as if he expected to see blood or broken bones.

Oh God. There could have been blood or broken bones. "I'm fine. Cold. Scared. But fine."

His brows dipped beneath the edge of his knit hat. "What the hell are you doing out in this weather?"

She bristled at his reprimanding tone. "I could ask you the same thing."

He huffed, then chuckled. "Point taken. Guess we both got surprised by the storm."

That was more like it. "Can you help get me out of here?"

"The car's buried too deep for my pickup to pull you out, but I can get you out of the cold. We'll go back to the Best Bay exit. I'll take you to my place 'til the storm lets up."

"What about my car?" Alone with Joe Waterman at his house? That was a bad idea. *Probably* a really bad idea. Talk about awkward. And tempting, because as soon as she saw him, all those old unwanted emotions rose from the ashes of her heart like a freaking phoenix. "Can't I call someone to pull it out?"

"Yeah, but it's not going to be tonight, honey. As long as we can get to safety, I'm not calling a wrecker out into this weather."

"Of course, you're right. It's just a car."

Honey? He called her honey? What did that mean? She gave herself a mental shake. It didn't have to mean anything. Gah, she felt like she was in high school again. Guys used endearments all the time. It didn't have to mean anything.

She and Joe had never even touched except for the occasional awkward hug, but she'd always felt guilty because she'd *wanted* to touch him – and not the way a friend would. But Joe would have never crossed that line. And neither would she.

She'd been married to his best friend.

TRUST ME – Silver Fox Romance book #3 – Coming in 2017

Home and family have always been the most important things to elementary teacher, Maggie Sheridan. When her daughter's marriage falls apart, Maggie offers to help watch her grandchildren. She's normally a quiet, glass-half-full kind of person, but when a trip to a local restaurant turns into a disaster, she finds herself giving the hot grumpy guy at the next table a piece of her mind.

Ben Krasinski's glass is usually half-empty. He's never had much patience for kids, but he thinks the redhead yelling at him is glorious. When she brings her car into his station for repairs, their banter quickly changes from bickering to flirting. Soon he's taking her on her first motorcycle ride and she has him playing catch with the kids in the backyard.

But when family interferes with their budding romance, can they trust each other enough to keep working at their relationship, or will they take the easy way out and walk away for good?

About the Author

Natasha Moore fell in love with the written word as soon as she could read. She writes sexy contemporary and erotic romance because she believes that stories of love and hope are important, and that there's nothing better than a happy ending. She's a snowbird, spending the winters in sunny Florida and the rest of the year in beautiful New York State with her real life hero who is happy to tell everyone that he's her inspiration. Visit her online at www.natashamoore.com, www.facebook.com/natashamooreauthor/ and www.twitter.com/natashamoore

Copyright

Choose Me

Cover by Lacey Savage

Made in the USA
Monee, IL
27 June 2022

98689875R00111